A Cowboy's Heart of Gold

SWEET VIEW RANCH
BOOK FOUR

JESSIE GUSSMAN

Contents

Acknowledgments

Cover art by Julia Gussman
Editing by Heather Hayden
Narration by Jay Dyess
Author Services by CE Author Assistant

Listen to the unabridged audio for FREE performed by Jay Dyess on the Say with Jay channel on YouTube. Get early access to all of Jay's recordings and listen to Jessie's books before they're available to the general public, plus get daily Bible readings by Jay and bonus scenes by becoming a Say with Jay channel member.

Chapter One

Her piglets were out.

Claudia Clybourn blinked in disbelief from the driver's seat of the old farm truck she had been driving down the main street of Sweet Water, North Dakota.

How had that happened?

Maybe they weren't her piglets. But a glance in the side mirror confirmed that the endgate of her trailer swung wide open.

Great. How was she going to round them up?

"I guess we're going to be chasing piglets for a little bit," she said, trying to keep the frustration out of her voice as she looked over at her dog, Ginger, who lay on the seat, and spoke to Mina, the young girl who was staying with her for the summer.

Claudia's friend, Olivia, from when she lived in Wyoming, was going through a hard time with her husband, and her mother had just been diagnosed with cancer. Olivia had been beside herself, trying to figure out how she was going to handle everything and also take care of her daughter who had just gotten out of school for summer break.

The last time Claudia had talked to her, Claudia had volunteered to let Mina come to the Sweet View Ranch for the summer.

Mina had been excited, and Olivia had jumped on the opportunity to send her daughter to someone she trusted and knew would take good care of her.

Olivia had just dropped Mina off the day before, and Claudia and Mina's first outing together was today to pick up piglets and bring them back to the Sweet View Ranch. They would make a great addition to their dude ranch for the summer, plus they'd be food for the winter.

Not that Claudia liked thinking that way, but it was a fact of life on the ranch.

Anyway, it was an inauspicious start.

"Awesome!" Mina said, jerking on her door handle and hopping out. At least Claudia couldn't complain that the girl wasn't eager to help.

She actually really liked Mina. She was a sweet girl and had a great attitude. Olivia had done a good job with her, although Claudia supposed that Mina had some things she was hiding. Nothing serious, just...her parents were going through a difficult time, which was always hard on children. So far, Mina hadn't said anything about it, but in Claudia's experience, kids processed those things deeply, and they came out at the oddest times.

Yanking on the old latch that stuck more than it didn't, she jumped out of the truck, waiting for Ginger, who moved rather slowly in her old age, to clamber out behind her.

Someday soon, Ginger wasn't going to wake up. Claudia didn't want to think about it, since Ginger had been a part of her life for more than half of it. She had ancestors who were herding animals, but her pedigree was so mixed, it was difficult to tell what breed she was.

She was at least eighteen years old and rarely did anything anymore besides walk outside to use the restroom twice a day. But she loved car rides, and when she had seen Claudia leaving this morning with Mina, her sad old eyes had begged Claudia to take her with her, and Claudia couldn't say no to the dog who had been her best friend in the world for so long.

Now, as she waited for Ginger to make her way out of the truck, she tried to figure out how in the world she was going to round up eight piglets. They seemed to be running all over the place.

"I guess we'll just try to sneak up on them and grab them," she said to Mina who had come around the truck and waited for instructions.

"All right." Mina started out, then she stopped and turned around. She was skinny, a typical twelve-year-old who hadn't started to fill out, all legs and arms and elbows and knees, with a big smile that shone with all the metal in her mouth. Olivia had warned Claudia when she dropped her off that Mina would need to go for several orthodontist appointments over the summer.

That meant a long, eight-hour drive back to Wyoming, but Claudia wouldn't mind. If her friend needed help, she would do her best. Of course, they were busy on the ranch, and Claudia was trying to start an orchestra in Sweet Water. Maybe not an orchestra, she would be happy with just a chamber ensemble, but she hadn't realized how expensive sheet music was, and she had spent a lot of long evenings applying for funding.

"What do I do when I catch them?" Mina asked, looking a little confused.

"I guess we'll throw them back in the trailer." Claudia didn't have any better ideas than that. Unfortunately.

Piglets were not exactly her area of expertise.

They hadn't had many of them over the years, because her dad hadn't liked them. He said they were impossible to keep in, they stunk, and the manure wasn't good for anything. And considering all of their downsides, he'd just as soon buy his bacon at the store.

But her parents had died in a car accident a decade ago, leaving her and her eleven siblings to first run the ranch in Wyoming and then the ranch they'd bought here in North Dakota.

There wasn't a day that went by that Claudia didn't miss her parents.

Ginger stood at her heels, and even though she was old and her joints were stiff and she barely did more than walk, she seemed eager at the idea of herding anything. It was an instinct that had been bred into her, and one she'd always taken great delight in using, whether it was cows, horses, pigs, or when they were little, Ginger had herded Claudia's younger siblings quite often.

Claudia remembered her mom getting rather frustrated at the dog who couldn't seem to tell the difference between an animal and a human. Although, they could let the kids out in the yard and didn't have to worry about anyone leaving, because if they tried, Ginger would herd them back in.

And with twelve children, Claudia figured that was actually a help rather than a hindrance. Although her mom had never said.

"There's one!" Mina said, zipping off after the piglet, her long, skinny legs churning. She had turned twelve in the spring but could easily pass for an eight-year-old.

As Mina took off after that one, Claudia saw another one scooting out from underneath a blue sedan. A sedan that looked an awful lot like Reverend Lewis's, pastor of the Sweet Water Methodist Church.

He wasn't exactly known for his patience, but he was known for caring a lot about his car.

Claudia tried to speed walk stealthily, which seemed like a contradiction of terms, toward the piglet.

Ginger walked stiffly at her side.

At least the streets of Sweet Water were deserted, she thought as she managed to get within two feet of the piglet before it saw her and took off in the opposite direction.

She felt like they were never going to get the piglets rounded up, but at least no one was going to witness her folly.

She thought too soon, as a dark green pickup, with tinted windows and familiar custom pipes, pulled into the end of town.

No. It was a rather distinctive truck, and Claudia wanted to drop through the pavement. No. Of all the people who could drive into Sweet Water at this time of day, it could not be Beau Hansen.

She hurried around the edge of Rev. Lewis's teal blue sedan, scrunching down and hoping that a piglet would run out in front of her, so in case anyone—Beau—saw her, it would look like she was actually doing something to help round the piglets up instead of hiding from Beau Hansen. But she was definitely hiding from Beau Hansen.

Except, Ginger didn't follow her. Ginger stayed at the back of the car and let out two loud barks. Almost as though she was telling Claudia that she was going the wrong way and she needed to turn around and get with the program. Ginger of course would be confused as to why

Claudia would be crouching down behind the car instead of chasing the piglets, which was so much more fun.

Even in her advanced age, it was obvious Ginger was eager to round up anything.

"Just give me a minute, okay, Ginger?"

Even to her dog, she didn't want to admit that she was hiding. But it seemed like every time she saw Beau Hansen, he had something unkind to say to her. They had butted heads since her family had first set foot in Sweet Water, eight years ago.

Sometimes in a person's life, there were people that they never got along with, and Beau was that person to Claudia. Odd, because Claudia didn't have a problem getting along with anyone else. As for Beau, she didn't really know. Although part of her wanted to say that he was a jerk to everyone, but she was pretty sure he was well respected in town, and she was the only one who couldn't get along with him.

But every time they bumped into each other, they traded insults, if not butted heads, literally. Since she had run into him and knocked him down the first or second time they met. It was a total accident, because she'd been carrying several large boxes of books she had intended to donate to Sweet Water's used bookstore and coffee shop, except she'd gone in the wrong door.

Understandable, since she couldn't really see anything around the boxes and wasn't familiar with Sweet Water, so as she came out of the grocery store, frustrated with herself because she'd gone in the wrong building, she'd been going a little too fast, hadn't been able to see where she was going, and ran straight into Beau, knocking him on his butt.

She hadn't laughed at the time, although she spent a good bit of time since smiling at the memory of him on the pavement, shock on his face as he looked up at her.

He seemed totally flabbergasted that anyone would dare step into his way, let alone touch him and knock him down.

He was arrogant and egotistical, and that was exactly the kind of thing Claudia could picture him thinking.

But she had been focused on balancing the boxes and laughed a little as the top one jiggled and then settled back down.

He assumed she was laughing at him and had said something

sarcastic. Which she had taken the complete wrong way, because she had been about to ask him if he was okay and offer to set the boxes down so she could help him up.

Anyway, the first meeting had gone rather poorly, and it was all her fault. But she never apologized, because any time she saw him after that, he was so busy insulting her, so by the time she was able to get her mouth open, she found herself insulting him back.

"Just be quiet. Please?" she hissed back at Ginger, not wanting Ginger to draw attention to her. Ginger was well-known around town, since Claudia seldom went to town without her. She wouldn't put it past Beau to see her dog, stop his pickup, and go looking for her, just so he could throw some insults at her and give himself something to smile about for the rest of the day.

He was so annoying.

"I got one!" Mina called from the front of the farm truck.

Squealing noises emphasized that she actually did have a hold on a hog.

"Come help me, please! I can't open the door and hold onto it at the same time. It wiggles too much!"

From through the windows of the car, she could see Beau's pickup was almost beside her. This just seemed to be the way her life seemed to turn out. Of course, she'd have to stand up from beside the car and walk in full view of Beau to the trailer, where she needed to open it.

It stunk, but short of leaving Mina high and dry, she didn't have a choice.

"I'm coming!"

"Is there one underneath the car?" Mina called out. Her voice sounded like she was struggling a bit with the piglet she held. They weren't that big, only about twenty pounds each, but still, twenty pounds of snout and legs and frightened wiggle was enough to keep anyone on their toes.

"Hurry up! I almost dropped it!"

Claudia stood up, careful not to look at the pickup which had slowed to almost a stop right beside Rev. Lewis's distinctive teal car. She could only hope that Beau had slowed because he was looking for a color change for his truck and not because he had seen her crouching down, hiding from him.

She hurried to the back of the trailer, where she pulled the endgate open so Mina could deposit her wiggling and squealing captive inside.

Chapter Two

Ginger had followed Claudia but stood just behind Rev. Lewis's car, looking at the pickup and wagging her tail slowly.

Her dog even acted friendly toward that man. Claudia wanted to disown her.

Not really. She loved Ginger way too much to disown her, but part of her love for Ginger was because of Ginger's loyalty.

"Ginger, he is not our friend," she muttered under her breath, just as the pickup shut off, right in the middle of the street, and the tinted window wound down, exposing a face that was way too handsome for its own good.

She wanted to be a good example for Mina, and she could tell that Mina was looking at her, so while she wanted to turn and walk in the opposite direction, she really couldn't.

Except, just then, a pig came squealing out from underneath the trailer, and both she and Mina turned and ran for it at the same time.

Mina lunged just as Claudia bent down to scoop it up. Claudia didn't want to run into Mina, so she swerved but didn't quite lift her foot high enough to get on the curb, and she ended up falling on her side on the hard cement sidewalk.

At least she hadn't fallen just a foot beside her, where there was a picnic bench and a streetlight. She would have hit her head or something. Not that the concrete was a soft landing, because she was pretty sure she had scraped her elbow. Funny how pain didn't really register when her sole purpose in life was getting away from Beau Hansen.

She scrambled to her feet, seeing that Mina had actually caught the pig and was holding it as it wiggled and squealed and tried as hard as its little body could to get away.

"I need the trailer open!" Mina said triumphantly. "I caught another one!" She grinned. "Two for me."

"Yeah. You're doing a great job," Claudia said, realizing that she had hit her hip in a weird way as well, and it hurt as she got up. She tried hard not to limp as she heard soft male laughter behind her.

Grrr. She wanted to wipe the smirk right off his face and shove his laughter back down his throat, but Mina was watching, and she needed to be a good example. So, no physical violence. Although, she allowed herself a few insults in thought only.

And immediately, she felt bad. It was hypocritical for her to put on a good show for Mina and yet allow her thoughts to be mean and unkind. It was no less of a sin, and she said a soft prayer of remorse.

Her thought life was her downfall. She could be kind on the outside, but her thoughts were often the opposite of what she actually acted.

She'd been struggling to get a hold of that for years, and it seemed like she had made no progress.

Still, acting kind, even if she didn't think kind thoughts, was better than being unkind all the way around.

She was only trying to justify her sin, and she knew that.

"Thank you," Mina said in a voice that sounded way too perky and happy for Claudia's mood. "Two down, six more to go! I'll call for you when I need you to open the endgate again."

Mina went running off to find another piglet.

She went up the street, and Claudia figured she should go the opposite direction, but she didn't want to, because that would mean turning around and coming almost face-to-face with Beau Hansen as he sat there in his pickup, probably staring and laughing.

So she turned and stepped up on the sidewalk.

"Good to see you actually can manage to take three steps without running into someone or falling down."

Why did such a nasty person have to have such an amazing voice? It was the kind of voice that made shivers run up and down her backbone. Even when he was insulting her.

She really, really hated it. Truly she did, except...she loved it too.

Deciding that if she ignored bullies they usually went away, she tried to pretend that she didn't hear a thing. And kept walking.

She took three steps before the voice came again, and it was just by her ear. "You're bleeding."

"I have six piglets running around town, and I need to catch them as soon as I can."

"You know, pigs will eat a human, if they think they can get away with it. That blood is going to make them go nuts and probably consume you in some kind of pack violence."

"They're twenty-pound piglets. I'm pretty sure I can handle them. Don't you have somewhere you have to be?"

She kept walking, not even bothering to look to see if there were any piglets around or trying to figure out where she should be going. She just wanted to get away from Beau.

"Pigs are filthy. That could get infected."

"And I will take care of it, as soon as I round up the other six pigs."

"Do you need some help?"

"Not from you!" She crossed her arms over her chest and turned to him, planting her feet and opening her mouth. "I heard you laughing. I'm pretty sure if you helped me, all you would do is chase them away from me just so you could sit there and have some kinda sick amusement for your day. Thank you. Just...leave."

Movement caught her eye, and she glanced around Beau, whose wide shoulders seemed to go on forever and ever, to see that one of her piglets had just chased another one of her piglets underneath his truck.

Great. That was exactly what she wanted to have happen. Not.

Without saying anything more to him, she reversed direction and brushed past, trying not to look as foolish as she felt as she power walked and crouched-snuck at the same time to where she could bend down and look underneath his truck.

"Are you trying to disable it so I'll be stuck in the middle of the street for the rest of the day?" he said, and it sounded like he was standing right behind her.

"No. I have two piglets under there. I'm going to try to get them." Then, since he really couldn't leave as long as her pigs were under his truck, she said, "If you want to make yourself helpful, go over to the other side and grab them when they come out."

She didn't expect him to actually do what she told him to. She was just trying to get him to shut up so she could concentrate. It was bad enough that she had to work in front of him. How was she supposed to concentrate when she knew he was making fun of her every move?

She just had to put him out of her mind, except putting Beau out of her mind when he was right there was next to impossible. She might as well pull out her wings and start flying around to catch the piglets.

So, it surprised her when she heard his footsteps move behind her, his cowboy boots making a clumping sound on the pavement as he walked around his truck.

It was a good thing Sweet Water was a small town, although there was typically truck traffic at different times of the day, since the Calhouns had a trucking company at one end of town and Baldwin's sale barn sat at the other end.

Regardless, God definitely blessed them with a quiet moment to grab their runaways, since there hadn't been a single car...except for Beau's.

She wasn't even sure he counted. She didn't want to count him anyway.

But still, it seemed like he was helping her, although she wouldn't put it past him to scare the pigs the whole way to Rockerton.

She didn't really trust him, but she had to let it go, because it needed to be done.

Bending down, she could see both piglets standing nose to nose underneath the truck.

"I'm over here, if you're going to scare them out."

That voice. Ugh. Why did it have to be Beau's voice that had that effect on her backbone? Why couldn't it be someone nice?

Regardless, she said, "Okay. I'm going to see what I can do." She scrunched down, unsure whether to be thankful that his truck did not sit low to the ground, or whether that was a curse, because she had enough room to roll underneath it.

When waving her hands at the piglets didn't work, she stretched out and managed to get her body under the running board and roll to her back.

She flapped her hand at the piglets, unable to roll again but hoping that they would think she was scary enough to take off out the other side.

Sure enough, her movements scared them, and they trotted out, right underneath Beau's stomach. He had crouched down on one knee and had been looking under the truck.

His laughter rang out at the same time the piglets started truly running.

"You missed them!" she said, frustration leaking out of her voice. She had slid the whole way underneath his truck, sacrificing her dignity, to get the piglets picked up, and all he could do was sit there and laugh at her?

She had accomplished her objective, and he had totally messed up.

"Sorry. You should have warned me that it was going to be humorous. After all, it's not every day that I get to see the dignified Claudia Clybourn sliding under my truck."

Dignified? It seemed like all she did when she was around him was land on her face.

"I got another one! I need the back open! Fast!" Mina called, which prompted Claudia to start struggling back out from under his truck.

She didn't bother to look to see if he was still kneeling down and laughing at her or not. She didn't care. At least that's what she told herself. She just needed to get the piglets.

She was so grateful that Mina had managed to get three.

There were only five more running around, although there would only be three if Beau had caught the ones that had just run underneath him, close enough for him to fall on top of.

By the time she had struggled out from under his truck, Beau was already opening the back of the trailer. Mina deposited her piglet inside and looked up at him with shining and happy eyes.

"Thanks! This is fun!" she said, trotting off back toward the front of the farm truck where she came from. "I saw another one up here. I'm going to grab it!" she called over her shoulder as she trotted away.

"Well, looks like the kid is doing better than you are. Whose kid is it anyway?" He paused. "Yours?"

"Yeah. She's mine," Claudia said, and she meant it to come out sarcastically, but she could tell she didn't succeed when Beau said, "I didn't know you had a kid."

She shrugged, not wanting to talk to him more than she needed to. "I also have piglets to pick up. Excuse me."

She felt bad, like maybe he had been holding out a bit of an olive branch, and she had brushed by it. But she was still annoyed that he had laughed at her, twice, plus her arm hurt from where she fell, her hip was burning, and she just crawled underneath his truck for no reason. "Maybe you'll want to get your truck out of the middle of the road," she muttered as she stomped away, trying to figure out where the two piglets that had been under his truck had gone.

"After I help you catch these piglets, I'll do just that. How'd they get loose anyway?"

"I don't know." She must not have latched the endgate tight when she picked them up at the pig farm on the other side of Rockerton. Although, she'd driven for an hour without it coming open, so maybe it had worked its way loose. Maybe she just hadn't shut it quite enough. She didn't typically haul things in the trailer, but eight twenty-pound piglets didn't seem like a big load, and it wasn't like hauling cattle or horses.

She considered herself a rather good driver, but she didn't have much experience with the trailer. She'd been the only one on the ranch that had been able to go, and they wanted to have the pigs there when the first guests arrived on Monday. They had a lot riding on their dude ranch being successful, and she had volunteered to go, just to try to be helpful. Even if it wasn't exactly her area.

Plus, it was a good opportunity for her and Mina to spend some time together and get to know each other. Two hours in the pickup together, and they could chat about anything. Mina wasn't shy. She was outgoing and friendly and chatted up a storm on the way there and the way back.

Obviously, she was a much better pig chaser than Claudia was, so it was a good thing she had her along.

Claudia started out across the street, looking both ways, even though they hadn't seen a single car since they stopped. God had been good that way. She just hoped that they could continue until they had caught all the piglets and no one ran over one or, worse, swerved to miss one and hit something they shouldn't.

"There's one!" Beau said from beside her.

She turned in the direction of his pointed finger and saw he was right.

"There are two," she corrected, hurrying in that direction.

"I'll get ahead of them, cut them off, and if they go back toward you, you can grab them, or I'll sneak up behind them."

She couldn't believe she was actually making plans with Beau. She still wanted him to leave, but she supposed she could use his help catching the piglets first.

"All right," she said as he hurried in front of her to cut the piglets off. They were just moseying down the street, like they were interested in their new surroundings and out for a stroll checking things out. Thankfully they weren't wildly running around, or they would have been long gone by now. Obviously, they were tame piglets.

"Hey, guys. Let's get back on the trailer. Although, I can't blame you for wanting to run away. I bet Miss Claudia has plans to eat you later."

"Would you stop?" she said. "Whose side are you on anyway?" She should have known that he would be on the pigs' side.

A cold nose shoved into her hand, and she looked down to see Ginger looking up at her. Back in her day, Ginger would have been running around, herding the pigs up, and they would have been able to gather all eight of them up without too much trouble at all. Now, while it was obvious that she wanted to help, she hadn't been able to.

"Oh, sweetie. I'm sorry."

"Heads-up!" Beau called, and Claudia glanced up just in time to see the pigs running directly toward her. At least they were running fairly close together, like they didn't want to lose each other.

Ginger crouched, although it was a slow crouch, but still. She moved stiffly from one side to the other as the piglets approached.

Claudia wasn't quite sure how Mina had managed to catch three, because she wasn't sure how to go about grabbing them. Did she jump on top of them? Bend over with her arms out?

Or was there some other technique she hadn't figured out?

She probably spent two seconds trying to figure that out, and by that time, the piglets had gotten to Ginger, who wasn't quite fast enough to turn them around, and they ran directly into Claudia's cowboy boots. She reached down with both hands, sticking her arms around the squirmy little bodies and picking them both up, one in each arm.

Unfortunately, the pigs were facing backward, and she was facing forward, and all she had to leverage them was to hold them tight against her hips.

She was afraid if she walked, they would jiggle loose.

"Mina!" she called.

"I have another one!" Mina called from up the street on the other side of the trailer, where Claudia could not see her.

"I kind of feel like I should be filming this, because I would have a viral video on my hands." Beau came over around the car, humor in his voice as he plucked one of the piglets from under her left arm.

That gave her the leverage to reach over and adjust the other piglet so that she didn't feel like she was going to drop it at any second.

"That would be something you would do, profit off of the suffering of someone else."

"You don't look like you're suffering all that much to me," he said with irony in his voice. "I think the piglets have it much worse."

"You told them I was going to eat them. That was not very nice of you." She had actually found that funny, but she didn't want to admit it.

She grabbed the end of the trailer, opening it wide enough to put the piglet she held inside, closing and then opening it so Beau could get his in.

"Thank you," she said, although the word came out reluctantly. Normally she didn't have a hard time telling people thanks or being grateful, but it was kind of rough being grateful to someone who she felt didn't like her very much at all and who would rather make fun of her and make her life miserable than anything.

"I have one!" Mina said, jogging up to the side of the trailer. Claudia opened the endgate and allowed her to throw it in.

"I think just two more, right?" Mina said. "Did you just put two in?"

"Yeah. If you've gotten four and we've gotten two, then there's just two more."

"All right! I never thought I would be good at chasing piglets, but it's kind of fun," Mina said, her voice chirpy and happy and her posture saying she was having the time of her life.

"She must have her father's personality, since she seems like your opposite. She's so happy," Beau said as Mina skipped away, and Claudia narrowed her eyes. "Where is the dad anyway?" His voice sounded studiously casual.

She wanted to tell him to mind his own business, but this was her opportunity to correct the misconception that he had before.

"She's the daughter of a friend of mine. She's staying with me for the summer. So there. None of my genes are interfering with her happy, sweet disposition."

"You know, if you tried, you'd probably be a really nice person." He sauntered off, and as though mocking her, he called, "Here, piggy, piggy, piggy. Here, piggy, piggy. Come on, bacon, bring your sausages over here."

He was such a dork.

She couldn't help laughing all the same. Except, she stifled it so he wouldn't know. She couldn't let him know that she actually thought he was...funny.

Odd, since she thought of him as rather serious and definitely a jerk. But he'd helped her round up her piglets, and she really couldn't complain about that.

She put a hand on Ginger's faithful head, and they followed him, Ginger and she both walking stiffly, Ginger with her tail up, like she was eager to continue to herd piglets.

And as though his calling had summoned a piglet, it strolled up the opposite sidewalk, like it had taken a little tour of the town and was ready to come back to the trailer.

She paused. Just her luck, he'd probably catch it by himself.

He went around behind the piglet. Maybe he had intended to chase it across the street to her, but Ginger headed it off. It turned around, and the piglet ran right into Beau's arms.

It was disgusting. Except, it was also a relief, because all the piglets were caught. She would have thought they would have been scattered to the four winds by now, and she did appreciate that the Lord had worked it out that they hadn't lost a single one.

"Mina!" she called up the sidewalk where Mina bent over, looking underneath a white pickup parked along the street in front of the diner. "He found it!"

"Nice! And I have the last one. That was fun!" she called, trotting back down the street holding a squealing piglet.

Ginger had come over and stood beside Claudia, and although she was a little put out with her dog for being disloyal, she couldn't be upset with Ginger for long. Ginger had been faithful her entire life.

They met at the back of the trailer as the last pig was loaded and the door closed.

"After all that work, wouldn't it be funny if they all got out again?" Beau said, and Claudia narrowed her eyes at him.

"That would not be funny. Do not even suggest such a thing."

"Are you gonna let me look at your arm?" he asked, although he didn't seem to hold out much hope that she would acquiesce.

She did not. He probably just wanted to scrape it even deeper.

"We'll take care of it when I get home. Thanks for your help." She forced herself to be kind. She could do this.

He jerked his head, gave a little grin to Mina, and said, "I think you might have a career as a pig wrestler. You're pretty good."

"Is there such a thing?" Mina asked, sounding interested.

"I don't know. But if there is, you'll be top notch." With another glance at Claudia, Beau walked back to his truck.

She did not wait to watch him get in but instead said to Mina, "Let's go. The folks at home are gonna wonder where we are."

Grateful that it hadn't taken that long, she went to the front of her truck, helped Ginger in, and started it. It was just her luck that Beau happened along, and as she looked in her side mirror, he blinked his lights at her, indicating she should pull out ahead of him.

She had a good mind to sit there until doomsday, making him go first, but that seemed a little childish. So, she put her turn signal on and pulled out.

"Oh!" Mina said almost immediately. "We missed one!"

But no, as she hit the brakes, the trailer door slammed against the trailer, and she realized that Beau must have unlatched it while he was standing there with his hand on it. Or maybe never latched it to begin with.

And as she watched in the mirror, all eight piglets filed out from behind the trailer and ran down the street of Sweet Water again.

She was going to be hard-pressed not to murder someone.

Chapter Three

Beau watched in horror as the endgate of Claudia's trailer swung open in front of him. He was glad he hadn't pulled out right away, or it would have hit his truck, but worse than that, all the piglets jumped back out and scattered along the streets of Sweet Water.

Claudia was going to die. Actually, more than likely, she was going to find a way to blame him. He wished he would never have said wouldn't it be funny if they all got out again. Surely she was going to take that as he had somehow figured out a way to open the gate and let all the pigs out. Like he would take some kind of sadistic pleasure in doing that.

Why did she always think the worst of him?

But he knew. He had deliberately teased her and provoked her, acting like a junior high boy around her for the longest time. The first time he'd seen her, he'd been overwhelmed. Intrigued. Unable to look away. But somehow, maybe it was because she ran into him the first time they actually met, their relationship had been rocky for years.

He didn't really know what to do to fix it, and somehow he managed to sabotage it every time he saw her and make it worse. This was going to go in that category. He was fairly certain.

He should keep driving. But that would make him look even more guilty. Plus, he didn't want to run over any pigs. So he stopped.

By the time he opened his door, Claudia had already come back with her hands on her hips, thunderclouds in her eyes, her old, decrepit dog at her heels.

"No." Her pointer finger came up and waved in the air. "Don't you even get out of your truck. You just get right back in there and drive on down the road. I do not need your 'help,'" she said, using air quotes around the word "help."

"Claudia. I promise. It wasn't me."

"Whatever. You expect me to believe that? When you were laughing about how funny it would be if they got out again? No. Just don't even. Honest-to-goodness, I don't think I can keep from punching you right in the nose if you even so much as set foot toward one of my piglets. Leave. Now."

She threw a hand out and pointed in the general direction away from town.

He didn't want to go. First of all, there was definitely something inside of him that rebelled at the idea of being bossed around and ordered about, like he was two instead of thirty.

Second, he hated to leave her there, alone, trying to pick up her piglets with just a little girl to help. Of course, there was her dog. Back in its heyday, her dog might have been a good help. Today, he wouldn't be surprised if the poor thing keeled over from all the excitement. But it wasn't going to be a help.

And third... Wherever she was, he felt drawn to her. He didn't want to give up the opportunity to continue to be with her. But he supposed that part of life was figuring out when to fold and wait for the next round.

"I'm telling you, it wasn't me." But he pressed his lips together and got back in his pickup, her still standing there with her arms akimbo as though to make sure he got in, started to back up, and drove away.

He had been going to the hardware store, and he pulled in the alley and parked in the lot behind the store, going in the back door.

He supposed if a pig went by, he would stop and pick it up, but he figured the best thing he could do was to stay out of her way.

Maybe he should let the idea of being friends with Claudia go. Every time she saw him, she avoided him like the plague. She wouldn't even talk to him in church, which, as a Christian, he figured that would be the one place where she would drop her animosity.

Of course, she'd never been rude; she just avoided him. When she saw him coming, she left whatever group she was in and walked to the other side of the building, even if she had to stand in a corner by herself to avoid him.

She did volunteer to work in the nursery, and he supposed he could corner her there, except...it would be a little odd for him to be hanging around the nursery. People would either assume, incorrectly, that he was there to steal someone's child or, correctly, that he was there because of his interest in Claudia. He really didn't want to be accused of either one, even though one was accurate.

"Good morning!" Mr. Strickland said as he glanced around and saw Beau coming in the back door.

Beau had grown up outside of Sweet Water on his parents' ranch, and he'd hung around the hardware store all of his life. Mr. Strickland didn't blink an eye at seeing him come in the back door.

"What can I do for you this morning?" Mr. Strickland said.

"I'm here to get a couple pounds of nails. We're fixing the chicken coop that blew over last winter."

"I know how your mom loves her chicks."

"Yeah. I have a few other odds and ends I need." He lifted a shoulder. "I can find everything on my own."

Mr. Strickland nodded and turned to another customer who was ready to check out.

Beau's phone rang, and he pulled it out of his pocket, glancing down to see that it was Adrian Winter, one of his buddies from college, who had become rather successful with his business in Bismarck.

"Hello?" Beau said, trying to remember the last time he talked to Adrian. It had been a couple of years at least.

"Hey, Beau. What's up?"

"Not much. Still on the ranch, still working. What about you?"

"Oh, business is going pretty well. The economy isn't great, but you can still make money if you know how, just not as much."

Beau laughed. "Well, that's good to know." People had to eat no matter how bad the economy was, but they would cut beef out of their grocery list, since it seemed to be more of a luxury item sometimes. "We're still in business, anyway."

"Yeah, I guess there's that." Adrian paused for a minute, and then he said, "So you're still in Sweet Water?"

"I am." That's where he'd been raised, and he loved North Dakota, with no intention of ever leaving.

"Good. I had an interesting request cross my desk this week, and I thought maybe I would give you a call, so we could both get a laugh out of it."

"Okay."

"Apparently there's someone in Sweet Water starting—hang on a second, let me look down at the exact wording they used in their email… a musical ensemble group." He laughed. "Really? In Sweet Water, North Dakota?"

Beau chuckled, although he wouldn't mind having a little culture in Sweet Water. It had grown, and it wasn't the tiny town that it used to be when he was a kid. The Olympic training center had a lot to do with that, plus the trucking company, the feed mill, and the auction barn had all grown and brought business to the town. According to his dad, Sweet Water was hardly recognizable from what it was when he had grown up. Still, if Adrian wanted to laugh about his small town and make fun of it, that was up to him.

Actually, if he recalled correctly, Claudia's family all played instruments. Beau forgot where he heard that, but occasionally he saw them play in church. Claudia herself played the viola. Of course, he had that knowledge tucked away.

"I don't know anything about it. But I guess this isn't the most likely place to have a musical ensemble."

"Certainly not." Adrian paused. "Get this. They wanted me to fund it. To donate funds, I guess I should say." He mentioned a figure, which didn't seem astronomically high to Beau. "There is no way I'm investing in any kind of musical ensemble in any town that has less than one hundred thousand people, and even then, I'd really be having an off day in order to think that that might present any type of return for me."

"Yeah. Were they asking for donations or were they asking for an investment?"

"I think the letter gave me the option of either one." He laughed, like that in itself was funny. "But I'm not interested in either. I figured I'd call and see if you knew what was going on. It seems...really odd."

"Who wrote the letter?" Beau asked, wondering which one of the old biddies in town had gotten some kind of weird idea in their mind. They were always doing crazy things. Right now, the big thing for the older folks in town was the swimming group they had up at the Olympic training center. It had started as a water aerobics class and had devolved into...Beau wasn't even sure. But he was glad that the folks kept themselves busy and figured when he got to be that age, he'd probably be looking for something to do too.

"It was signed by a Claudia Clybourn. Do you know her?"

Beau froze in front of a tempting display of propane torches.

Claudia wanted to start a musical group?

He had no idea. Of course he knew she played the viola, but...did he hear that she had gone to college for music? Maybe he had. Or maybe he'd heard that one of the Clybourns had. It must have been Claudia.

Still, that was crazy. He...had no idea. He was proficient on the French horn. Although he hadn't played in years, he thought that maybe this was his chance to support Claudia. She didn't even really need to know. He wasn't trying to do it to earn brownie points, exactly. He just really thought a lot of her and wanted to see her succeed.

He spoke into the silence that followed Adrian's laughter.

"I actually do know her. And she's a great girl. Tell you what," he said, pausing because he knew that if Adrian found all of that hilarious, he was going to find this even more funny, and Beau didn't know how to explain why he was going to say what he was going to say, and Adrian was going to draw a conclusion that...probably was more accurate than Beau wanted to admit it was.

"What?" Adrian prompted when Beau paused.

"I'll send you that amount, actually double that amount. And you can tell her it will be a monthly thing. You don't have to tell her you're doing it, you just can't tell her that I am."

There was silence before Adrian huffed out a laugh. But he sobered right away. "Are you serious?"

"Yeah. We are...well, you could call us adversaries. Enemies, I guess. But it makes me uncomfortable to not be getting along with her. Although, I'm not ready to tell her that, and she probably would refuse the money if she knew it was coming from me."

"All right. I didn't realize you were so interested in music."

He had just gotten a lot more interested in music than he had been in his life before.

"Yeah. I didn't know it either."

Adrian laughed. "All right. I guess I can do that, although I'll have to figure out how to get my secretary to word it so I'm not telling her the money is coming from me. Although it will be coming from me. All right. That's a little more complicated than I want to deal with, but I'll put my secretary on it."

"Thanks." He got Adrian's information so Beau could send him the money, and then they chatted for just a bit before they hung up.

Beau browsed around the store, getting the things that were on his list, thinking about Claudia. Starting a musical ensemble. Too bad he didn't play a stringed instrument, because he would join.

Just to give her a hard time. He kind of enjoyed their antagonistic interactions. She got so angry, it was almost funny.

Of course, she knew how to pull his strings too, although she hadn't done it today. He'd been having a good time. He thought she enjoyed it as well, but he probably would never find out. It was like they weren't ever going to have a civil conversation.

He walked to the counter to check out, and as he was chatting with Mr. Strickland, he noticed a sheet on the bulletin board which he'd missed earlier. It said, "musical ensemble starting soon. First meeting at the white church on Saturday, May 2, at 4 o'clock in the afternoon. Refreshments following."

Refreshments. Well, that was enough to catch his interest.

And it didn't say just stringed instruments. Maybe he would have to dust off his French horn and head to the church on Saturday. If nothing else, it would be interesting.

Chapter Four

"I probably owe him an apology," Claudia said as she leaned against the fence with her sister-in-law, Alaska, who had brought her children out to check out the new piglets.

Mina had fallen in love with Alaska's children when she arrived yesterday, and she held the baby, Alice, in one arm while she held Eugene's hand. They had crouched down nearby, and Eugene put his hands through the slats, trying to pet the babies.

"Were you that unkind to him?" Alaska asked, surprise in her voice. Claudia wasn't exactly known as someone who flew off the handle and went ballistic over little things. Of course, losing an entire load of piglets wasn't exactly a little thing, but it still wasn't the kind of thing that Claudia typically got upset over.

"Yeah. I was pretty harsh."

"Then, yeah, you should apologize. Obviously after Tobias checked out the endgate and saw that the latch had broken... He certainly didn't open it on purpose. I wouldn't have believed that to begin with. I mean, I know that your parents don't necessarily determine whether or not you're going to turn out well, but I would have thought that Ford and Morgan Hansen's son would be a respectful person."

"He generally has that kind of reputation around town. I mean, everyone thinks well of him. I seem to be the only person that can't get along with him. And to be fair to myself, he has been unkind to me in the past."

"It's funny how sometimes people just rub each other the wrong way." Alaska's finger tapped on the fence post as though she were trying to think about whether or not she should continue to talk.

"Go ahead and tell me. I need to be a better Christian because Christians are kind, even when they don't necessarily like the other person, and Jesus knows that we're Christians by our love, especially for our fellow Christians, and Beau is, apparently, a Christian as well, although I have trouble seeing that." She knew that last bit was not true or kind, and she wished she wouldn't have said it, but when it came to Beau, the insults just seemed to roll off her tongue without her even thinking about it. It made her wonder what exactly was in her mind, because she didn't think she had those mean thoughts there.

"I actually wasn't going to say anything of the kind. I was going to say...sometimes opposites attract. Sometimes attraction masks itself as antagonism. Just be careful," she said with a teasing smile.

Maybe she knew that was going to get Claudia's dander up, not in a necessarily bad way, just in a she really felt like she had to defend herself kind of way.

"That is one thing that will never happen. I do not find Beau Hansen the slightest bit attractive, and I guarantee you he does not see me like that either."

"Then why did he stop and help to begin with?"

"Because he saw a great opportunity to make fun of me, that's why! I mean, can you imagine all the jokes he's telling his friends right this very second? How often do you see someone chasing piglets around town? I can just hear me being called the hog chaser, the swine woman, the pig caller, the woman who can't keep her pigs in a line... I bet you this will hang on so long that all the people in Sweet Water will call me Pig Lady until my dying day."

"I feel like you're being just a little bit dramatic. Which is really not like you," Alaska said, her eyes sincere as she looked at Claudia, as though begging her to consider how she was acting and try to straighten up a little.

Alaska was right. Whether that was her intent or not, Claudia was being dramatic. And she did need to straighten up.

"Thank you for not commiserating with me. Thank you for telling me that I needed to be better. Sometimes it's hard to make yourself do right when everyone around you is telling you how right you are to do wrong."

"I don't think that's going to be a problem in this family. I have yet to have anyone pat my back and tell me that it's okay to be a sinner."

Claudia reached over, patted Alaska's back, and said, "It's okay to be a sinner. God expects that from us. But He also expects us to follow Jesus and try to live like him. Even though He doesn't expect us to be perfect."

"I couldn't have said it better," Alaska said as she looked at the tattoo sleeves on her arms, like she was thinking about her past life. They had to be a daily reminder of where she had been. It made Claudia very cautious about what kind of permanent marking she wanted to put on her own body.

"Mama! Look at this!" Eugene called, crouched beside a piglet who had come over to the fence and allowed them to scratch its back. It looked like it was really enjoying the ministrations.

"Well! It looks like she likes you."

"I like her!" He turned to Mina. "Is it a girl?"

Claudia smiled at the adorable little boy. He had certainly made life more interesting on the ranch. Not that living with her siblings hadn't made life interesting. It certainly had. They all had their fair share of drama in their lives. But she wouldn't change her life for anything. She loved that she got to get up and do what she loved every day, and she got to do it with people she loved as well.

Of course, she wouldn't mind being married, finding someone to spend her life with, to bring into her family. But a lot of men might be intimidated by her family or, worse, want her to leave them, although that was probably the right thing. After all, the man was the head of the home, and as a woman, God had created her to be his helper.

Still, ideally, she would find someone who would move to her farm and be a blessing to her family.

It wasn't that she would not consider anyone who wouldn't, but she just wasn't looking for that.

"How are things going with your music ensemble? Have you had anyone join?" Alaska asked as she turned back away from Mina and Eugene.

"I had a few people call me. But I probably won't know exactly how many I have until I get to the church on Saturday. But it might be a no go. I haven't heard whether or not I have any funding. And the music is so expensive. I've... I've thought about writing parts myself, but it will take forever. And I don't have that kind of time. It was already a stretch to carve out some time for practices."

"Yeah. There's always something to do here on the ranch. But if you put it on the shelf for this summer, you could spend the winter when we're not as busy writing the parts. Although I don't exactly know what you mean by that."

"Well, I need to have a flute part, and several violin parts and a horn part, or whatever kind of instruments we have, and a lot of them are in different keys. So music that would work for a flute, for example, wouldn't work for a trombone. But it would work for a violin. But a viola part is usually written in the key of C or alto clef."

"I'm sorry. You have totally lost me."

"I'm sorry. I get a little passionate about it, although my family makes fun of me because I went to school and got a degree in music education, and I haven't used that degree one day in my entire life. It was the biggest waste of money ever, except...I really enjoyed my studies. I mean, I guess I don't believe you should go to college to have fun. Going to college should be about getting an education and learning a trade, learning how to do the job that you're supposed to be able to do whenever you graduate. But my classes were so interesting, so much fun. I mean, after ranching, music is my love."

"It's always good to love something that makes you money."

"I guess I probably need to find a third love, then, since neither ranching nor music has a tendency to make anyone any money, ever."

They laughed together, and Claudia appreciated the fact that while

Alaska was new to the family, she felt so at ease with her that it was like they had known each other for longer. Of course, she would have expected Ezra to find a woman who was perfect for their family. Actually, knowing Ezra, God showed him exactly who he was supposed to marry, and Ezra did it.

The only thing was, it was obvious that Ezra was completely infatuated with his wife. He absolutely adored her, and Claudia was so happy to see her big brother with someone that he loved so deeply.

They were cute together too. They looked like complete opposites, but they had so much respect and love between them that a person forgot how different they were, and more than one person had commented on what a perfect match they made.

Of course, it meant that Ezra had moved out of the large farmhouse, which left a bit of a hole. But Claudia knew she probably ought to get ready for more of that. Surely now that they were settled in North Dakota, her siblings would start getting married. Almost all of them had waited to get married, just because of the instability of their family and ranch, then because of losing their parents, although Priscilla had had a disastrous attempt.

Thinking about Priscilla made her sad, and she turned her thoughts to hoping that someone would come through with money for her orchestra. If not, she would probably end up doing what Alaska said, which was put it off for a year until she could write music that they could use. It disappointed her though, because she really thought having a little bit of the arts in town would be a boon for their dude ranch. Surely their guests would want to go into town to enjoy good entertainment.

That was assuming that she would be a good enough director to actually make the ragtag group that she was sure was going to show up into some semblance of "good."

"All right. I probably ought to take my children and put them down for a nap. If I don't do it now, I'm going to regret it in a few hours when both of them are miserable, and I'll be miserable too."

"Well then, by all means, take the children and put them down," Claudia said, laughing.

She looked around for her dog. Ginger had probably overdone it with all the excitement over the pigs being out. Claudia should have made the dog stay in the truck. She knew that Ginger's working days were over. The problem was, Ginger didn't know it.

She wondered if that's what getting old was. Wanting to do things that she could no longer do.

Was there a way to combat that? Could she figure out how to have new interests and activities?

She figured she was probably the only person in her thirties who wondered what in the world she was going to do when she was in her eighties, but she always liked to be prepared.

"It's okay if I go help put the kids down?" Mina asked.

"Sure," Claudia said, glad that Mina had found something that made her happy. Of course, Mina was pretty much happy all the time. But being on the ranch kept her from thinking about what she might be missing at home.

"I'll be in in a little bit. Maybe we'll grab a snack since we missed lunch."

"All right," Mina said as she walked off with Alaska and the children.

Her dog was nowhere in sight, and Claudia wondered if maybe she'd fallen asleep in the pickup. It wasn't that warm out, but with the sun shining, it could get warm, especially in a closed cab.

Ginger wasn't exactly her dog. She was a farm dog, but from the time she'd been a pup, Claudia was the one who had taken care of her, and Ginger had chosen to be with Claudia if she wasn't needed somewhere else.

So, while she didn't technically belong to Claudia, Claudia was the one who usually spent the most time with her. She could have gone off anywhere. It wasn't that she never did, she just typically didn't.

Especially now that she was older.

Looking around, wondering where she'd find her dog, she hadn't quite figured out which direction to start looking when her phone buzzed in her pocket and she pulled it out.

It was a number she didn't recognize, and with her brows furrowed, she swiped and put it to her ear.

"Hello?"

"May I speak with Claudia Clybourn, please?" a friendly female voice said.

"This is she."

"Claudia. I am calling you on behalf of my boss, Adrian Winter. You had sent him an email requesting funds for your orchestra."

"Yes." Claudia tried to keep the hope out of her voice. She already had four emails declining her request in the last week. She had a couple the week before, and a few people hadn't responded at all.

She had a feeling she'd done something else that people were laughing at her for. It seemed like she provided a lot of entertainment for people over the years.

"My boss wanted me to call and let you know that you will be receiving a monthly donation toward your musical ensemble." The woman named a sum, which was far more than Claudia had hoped to get with all of the donations combined. Considering that it was her first and, if she was being honest, likely her only source of donation, she was over-the-moon excited.

She tried to sound professional when she said, "That's... That's fantastic. Please tell him thank you!"

She knew she was glowing, but she couldn't help it. She had been thinking like Alaska said, she was going to have to cancel her orchestra, and this... This would enable her to order pretty much whatever sheet music she wanted to.

Her mind had taken off, galloping in all kinds of directions with all the things that she would now be able to do, and she barely heard the lady ask for her financial info so they could send the money electronically.

The lady said that she would be sending an email as a follow-up.

Claudia was only too happy to give her that info, and by the time she hung up, she felt like she was practically levitating.

But as she tried to pull her mind back to reality, she suddenly realized that the way the woman had phrased everything didn't really disclose who the money was actually coming from. But, that was just splitting hairs, right? Just because she didn't say the money was coming from her boss...she'd said, "you will be receiving a monthly donation" but had not gone on to add that it would be from her boss. That was probably implied. Right?

She shook her head, reminding herself not to look a gift horse in the mouth. She still had work to do, the least of which was to try to find something that would work as a feed and water trough for the piglets. She wasn't done with that job yet. And then she had to think some more about the apology that she needed to issue to Beau.

She cringed at the idea. It was...a blow to her pride to admit that she had been wrong. But Tobias had been clear that the latch had been broken, and she had just been very, very lucky that the gate hadn't swung open again on the way home. He said it had something to do with the spring or something, that it was weak or something, so it only held part of the time.

Whatever it was, he'd driven the truck and trailer into the shop so that he could weld it or do whatever it was that he was going to do to fix it. Claudia had never learned to fix things the way her brothers had, with Tobias being one of the best. He could work on metal and wood and did well with both. If something needed to be fixed, Tobias was always her first choice. Although the other boys could do it in a pinch.

"Ginger!" she called, looking around the shed where they made the makeshift pen for the piglets. "Ginger!"

Things were almost ready for their first dude ranch visitors on Monday. Maybe she shouldn't have tried to start her orchestra at the same time, because it just added to her workload, but it did feel good to finally put her degree to use a little.

As she moved around the pen, she thought she saw white fur. Ginger was spotted, with what might have been blue heeler ancestry coming out in her markings. Certainly her ability to herd animals had come from somewhere, and a blue heeler was as good a choice as any.

Claudia had always thought she was so pretty and uniquely marked.

"Ginger," she said cheerfully as she saw that it was indeed Ginger lying on the other side of the pen.

She was so old that she probably didn't realize Claudia was ready to leave.

"Come on, Ginger. Let's head to the house. I bet you're thirsty."

She might have already gotten a drink from one of the water troughs around the barn, although she was probably exhausted from all of the exertion of the day.

But Ginger didn't move.

"Ginger," she said again. Realization was beginning to dawn, and her voice didn't sound quite as cheerful.

She walked slowly toward her dog, staring at her as she did so, trying to see her side go up and down with her breathing, but there was no movement.

Claudia knelt down, one hand on her dog's chest, and she knew immediately, from the stiffness under her fingers, that Ginger was no longer with her.

Why hadn't she paid attention to her when she came home? She could have spent her last few minutes sitting beside her, comforting her as she left this world. Instead, Ginger died alone.

She shook her head. She didn't need to be dramatic. Ginger died where she wanted to. And Claudia had been standing less than four feet away from her, which would have made Ginger very happy. She was near her mistress and had found a private place to depart.

She hadn't suffered it all. Beyond the normal arthritis and aches and pains that went with old age, old age of any mammal. Including humans. Someday Claudia's limbs would feel that way.

She took a breath and blew it out. She didn't really want to cry. She hated to cry. She was so miserable when she was crying, but...she loved her dog.

Ginger's eyes were closed, and she looked like she was sleeping. Claudia ran a hand down her neck and over her side, the familiar fur soft under her fingers.

She dropped her head as tears seeped out from underneath her eyelids. She didn't want to cry, but it was okay to be sad. It was okay to mourn losing a good friend. A friend who had been with her from her early teen years until now. They'd spent so much time together. Done so many things, and whether she was happy or sad, Ginger was beside her, licking her hand, telling her it was okay, letting her know she had a friend no matter what. She had been more loyal to Claudia than any of her real-life friends. She supposed that was a dog's job in life, just to be a friend.

She swallowed and brushed at her eyes, thinking about where she wanted to bury her dog.

She... She needed to look at music, she needed to get a trough for the pigs, a snack for Mina, and she had a whole list of other things she needed to do.

But right now, she just needed to take a minute and cry. To mourn the loss of her friend. And take care of her. That was the first thing.

Chapter Five

Beau pulled the saddle off the back of his horse and threw it on the rack attached to the barn wall.

He went back and grabbed the saddle pad, and put it upside down over the saddle so it would dry out.

Then he grabbed the brush and started grooming his horse.

He had just ridden out with his dad to check the herd. His dad was a successful businessman, and Beau was obviously aware of that. But his dad had also allowed Beau to choose what he wanted to do in his life, and while Beau had learned all of the business that Ford had thought important to teach, his true love lay with the land and the animals and their ranch.

He'd been working on it since he was old enough to put a coat on and go outside. His mom had supported his dad in thinking that their kids needed to learn to work as early as possible. And to enjoy it. And he thought that that was probably one of the most valuable things that his parents had taught him. To love to work.

He wasn't quite sure how they had managed to instill that in him, but they had. He and his two sisters all enjoyed working on the ranch, although his sisters had married and now had homes and families of their own, and whether or not they would ever come back to Sweet Water or live near their childhood home was up in the air.

As for him, there was no doubt where he wanted to be. Right where he was.

His dad had gotten a business call he needed to take, so Beau had taken his horse to the barn and said he would take care of brushing them both down.

It was a job he loved anyway. As much as he loved being on the back of his horse, checking herds, being out in the great outdoors, he also enjoyed the soothing motions of grooming. It was relaxing, not just for the horse, but for himself, and it gave him plenty of time to think.

He and Claudia had gotten off to a bad start years ago. And over the years, he'd come to admire her but had never been able to say so. He... might even feel more for her, but she refused to see him as anything but her enemy. Her adversary. And while he had to take responsibility for teasing her and picking on her, he wanted to change that.

He intended to put a few things in motion and hoped that perhaps she would eventually see he wasn't quite as monstrous as what he led her to believe over the years.

Thunder rumbled in the distance, and he was glad they had finished their ride. His dad wasn't exactly old, but he was getting up there, and the last thing he needed was to be riding in the rain, especially during a thunderstorm. That would be dangerous for both of them.

His dad didn't typically give him a hard time, but every once in a while, his mom would ask him when he was planning on settling down. If a man had hit his thirties and wasn't happily married with few kids, people started to think that they needed to start meddling with his life.

It was hard to explain to his parents that he had big shoes to fill. They had both been so successful, they both were such great examples to him, that he didn't want to mess up his life.

Also, he didn't want to spend the rest of his life with someone who was maybe pretty, even beautiful, or perhaps he was attracted to, but who didn't have the kind of character that would keep her with him through all of the things that life would throw at them.

He'd known that much from the time he was young, as he watched the dedication that his parents had toward each other. That's what he wanted for his own life, that…that elusive thing that made marriages seem to grow stronger and better through the years.

He hadn't been that smart when he was younger. He'd been too busy working and trying to make his parents proud of him, even though he knew they would be proud of him no matter what he did. But thankfully, that had occupied his time, and he hadn't gotten distracted with any one particular girl and hadn't ended up marrying the wrong one.

When he'd seen Claudia, he'd known almost immediately that she was different. At least for him. He'd prayed about it over the years, but God had not worked. Of course, God hadn't worked in any other areas either, and now… It seemed like maybe a door was cracking open just a bit. Maybe, it was just because he was forcing it.

Hero's tail swished, and Beau ran the brush down over his hindquarters. He hadn't gotten hot, since they'd just walked most of the way, and he hadn't needed to walk him to cool him down.

His phone buzzed, and he ran the brush across Hero's back several more times before he pulled it out of his pocket to read the text.

Her dog died.

That was all it said, but Beau knew exactly who he was talking about.

A name didn't come up on his phone, but he knew who had sent the message too.

Maybe this was an underhanded tactic, but Beau considered Tobias a friend, even a good friend. They talked about ranching and cows and work, though, and he never had talked about Claudia with him.

But about a month before when they had been bidding on the same lot of calves at the sale barn, and after Tobias had won, Beau had gone over to shake his hand. Tobias had given him one of his rare smiles, maybe because Tobias knew that Beau could outbid him all day long but had chosen to quit.

Beau wasn't sure, but he and Tobias had spent a good bit of time talking. Mostly about farming as they usually did, but before he had left the sale barn, he had mentioned Claudia and his dilemma. How she viewed him as an adversary, and how he wanted to change that. He had...uncharacteristically asked Tobias if he would help him.

Tobias had jerked his head at the time but hadn't verbally agreed or disagreed.

Beau had gone home feeling like an idiot. He didn't get that personal with any of his friends, and felt that he'd been maybe pushing to be more in Tobias's sister's life than Tobias felt he deserved. He wasn't sure. But he had gotten a text from Tobias two weeks later that said:

I'll help.

Then, that morning, Tobias had sent another simple text:

She's hauling piglets. The latch on the trailer
is almost broken.

He wasn't exactly sure what he was supposed to do with that information, but he had been in the right place at the right time, because he'd been able to help her gather them up. But then she thought he deliberately let them out.

He should have known better than to touch the endgate, knowing that the latch was no good. He had been waiting for an opportunity to tell her that he noticed that the latch was broken and be a help to her, instead of being blamed as the reason the piglets were running all over the place for a second time.

He managed to screw that up. He couldn't believe Tobias was helping him again. Except, it didn't really make him happy to hear that the old dog that had been with her had died.

It had been obvious that there had been a bond between the two of them, a bond that was maybe unusual between a human and their animal.

Beau blew out a breath. He couldn't go visit her. And as much as he'd like to offer to dig the grave, he doubted that would go over very well either. Not after earlier. She was liable to run away from him the second she saw him come onto the ranch.

But he knew what he could do. And putting the brush down and pulling up the Internet, he started doing it.

Chapter Six

Claudia stood in the rain, looking at the mound of dirt in front of her.

She had covered Ginger with a sack in the barn, and then she had gone and gotten Mina, and they got a snack, although Claudia had not eaten. Then, they'd gone out to the barn and gotten a water and feed trough set up for the piglets.

After that, Mina had gone in to help with the kids as they got up from their naps, and Claudia had gone off to one of her favorite spots on the farm. It was a little knoll, slightly higher than the ground around it. There were several trees growing there that provided some shade for the animals and shelter from the wind. It was rather unusual in North Dakota, since trees were sparse. But maybe that's what made the spot more special for her. That, and the little rise made it so that they could see even further than normal. Regardless, she'd taken a shovel and a digging iron and had dug the grave.

It seemed fitting that it had started to rain as she worked the ground. Maybe it was the Lord, because the rain suited her mood, and it also made the dirt easier to dig up. It also washed away the tears from her cheeks. Or at least blended in with them.

She'd gotten the hole to the point where it was more than waist deep, and then she pulled back the burlap sack and looked at Ginger's sweet, old face one more time.

She'd placed Ginger on the back of the four-wheeler, where she loved to ride any time they were doing anything anywhere over the ranch. Probably riding on the four-wheeler was her absolute favorite thing to do, after chasing cattle, of course.

They spent hours on the four-wheeler together, and the faster they went, the better Ginger liked it.

This last ride had been slow though. Claudia had needed it to be. She didn't want to go out and dig a hole for her dog, and she didn't want to admit that that part of her life was over and that she had to tell her friend goodbye.

She supposed that was the way it was at all funerals. Although at least humans had the hope of seeing their loved ones in heaven.

The Bible didn't mention an afterlife for dogs at all. Not in heaven, not anywhere. Of course, she wanted to believe that she would see Ginger again, but she had remembered searching Scripture for a glimpse of what happened to animals after they died back when she was in her early twenties, and she lost her favorite horse, and she hadn't found a thing.

There were horses in the battle of Armageddon, and perhaps her horses would be among that number, but again, the Bible just didn't say.

It was one of those things that she would just have to wait until she got to heaven before she found out. She really hoped her dog would be there. But it just wasn't something that she was going to know in this life.

The Bible did say that humans were made in the image of God, and that made them special. Humans had a soul, an eternal soul, and Jesus had died for them. Humans had been put in dominion over the animals and commanded to take care of them. That was all she knew.

She ran a hand down the still, wet muzzle as the rain mingled with the teardrops on her face. There was thunder in the distance, but the electrical part of the storm had passed, leaving a steady drizzle behind it.

Her siblings knew that her dog died, and Phoebe had offered to come with her, but she had shaken her head and said that she would prefer to be alone, although she had told her where Ginger lay in the barn, in case any of them wanted to say goodbye.

There were several other dogs on the ranch, but Ginger was special if only because she was the oldest.

She figured all of her siblings had probably taken a minute to go and pay their last respects, although she hadn't seen any of them. And they honored her wishes to be able to bury her alone.

She supposed there were people who would have wanted to have others around them, to have help, and to do it as a group, but Claudia appreciated having those last few minutes alone with her dog.

She couldn't really remember when she had gotten too old to help with the herding. It happened gradually, where after a day of working cattle, Ginger had been stiff for a few days. And then, she'd been stiff all the time. And then, she quit running.

Maybe it had just been in the last year or two that she had only really been able to wag her tail and crouch down, but springing up and cutting from one side to the other were things of the past.

It was probably better this way, and she liked to picture Ginger in her mind, running in the fields of heaven, even if it wasn't so. It made her happy.

She put her arms under her dog, already soaking wet, and carefully arranged the burlap sack so that it wrapped around her.

It really didn't matter, she supposed, but it made her feel better to think that her dog was protected so the dirt wasn't touching her. Ginger had been very meticulous about staying clean, although when it came to chasing animals, she was all in, and it didn't matter how dirty she got. Any other time, she was like a little princess keeping her paws out of the mud and making sure that her fluffy fur was groomed daily.

Claudia didn't say anything. It didn't seem like it mattered whether her words were in the air or just in her head. And so she just thought about what a good dog Ginger had been, and she thanked God for allowing her such a long time with her friend.

Kneeling in the mud, she carefully placed her dog in the hole she'd made, and then the burlap sack slowly started to disappear as she threw dirt on top of it.

It was a muddy mess by the time she was done, and her heart hurt. She supposed it probably would for a while.

Putting the shovel and the digging iron on the four-wheeler and securing them so they wouldn't roll off, she climbed on and motored slowly home.

The sun had come out by the time she arrived at the barn, and while she normally loved the way the earth smelled freshly washed after a storm, she barely noticed it. She put the shovel and digging iron away and walked into the house, ready for a shower.

A large bouquet of flowers sat on the kitchen table as she walked in the back door, and it made her smile a little as she tiptoed across the floor, trying not to drip.

"Those are for you," Alaska said, standing at the stove with Eugene playing at her feet.

Claudia stopped. "Flowers?" she said, surprised for some reason that her voice still worked, although it sounded rusty.

"Yeah. They came this afternoon."

Figuring that her brothers had gone together to do something nice for her, she smiled a little, even if it was a sad smile, and reached for the card.

The flowers were beautiful, cheerful, and they somehow reminded her of Ginger. Maybe it was because there were a few with an orange tint. Ginger had more the coloring of a blue heeler, but she supposed her name Ginger had always made her think of orange when she thought of her dog.

Regardless, the flowers looked perfect, and they definitely lit up the room.

She changed her mind about reading the card, since she didn't want to stand in the house, dirty, dripping, and unable to control her crying, and just grabbed the vase.

"I think I'll take them to my room," she said, thinking that while she loved them in the kitchen, she might need them tonight, because Ginger had always slept on her bed.

"I think they'll look perfect in your bedroom. And they'll be cheerful this evening for you when you're alone."

She nodded at Alaska and then carried the heavy vase out of the room with her and up the stairs.

She almost forgot that she was cold and wet and had mud splattered on her jeans as she set the vase down on her dresser and pulled out the card.

Her brothers would probably say something funny, although they might be serious for this occasion, just out of respect for her feelings. They wouldn't want to make her feel worse than what she did. For sure.

But it wasn't signed by her brothers.

Her brows furrowed as she read the note again.

Sorry about Ginger. I thought these might make you smile. — B

None of her brothers' names began with B.

None of her friends' names began with B.

Maybe it was Bernadine, one of the ladies in town who had been organizing the older ladies at the aquatics class at the Olympic training center.

It could possibly be her. But she was coming up empty on figuring out anyone else. Maybe she could ask around.

In the meantime, she took a shower, her heart heavy, her steps slow. But her tears were dried up at least. Until she came back in the room and thought about Ginger and how she loved to lie at the foot of the bed and kept Claudia's feet warm at night.

She hadn't been through a winter in eighteen years without Ginger on her feet keeping them warm.

Maybe she needed to invest in some wool socks. Although, part of her wanted to go get another dog right away. Except, there would never be another dog like Ginger, and she didn't want to be unfair to a new puppy, expecting it to be everything Ginger had been.

Her eyes landed on the flowers, and they made her smile. Their bright happiness, the thoughtfulness of whoever had sent them, someone who had known that her dog died. They had to have good contacts too, since she'd been just fine this morning in town.

Whoever it was, she appreciated it. It was a thoughtful gesture that she hadn't been expecting, and if the person had truly wanted to make her smile, they had been successful.

She took another look at the flowers as she had a hand on her knob to walk out of her room. She did not feel like going down and eating with her family, but she didn't want them up here, worried about her either.

Deciding that she would lie down on her bed for just a few minutes, she arranged the flowers so that she could lie and look at them, and before she realized it, she was asleep.

The next day, she woke groggy, confused, since she was still wearing her clothes and lying on top of her covers. She saw the flowers, smiled, and then she remembered.

The heartache wasn't quite as bad today as it had been yesterday. Maybe part of her had been hoping that she would wake up and it would all be a bad dream, but no such luck.

After getting dressed, and going out and doing her morning chores, she came in to see their neighbor, Ellen, in the kitchen with Alaska.

"Good morning," Alaska said with a tentative smile.

"Good morning," Claudia said, trying to make her smile look real and happy. She wasn't going to go around moping just because she lost her dog. She really didn't want to waste any of her life being sad. Although, she did think it was okay to feel sad when bad things happened. She just didn't want to wallow in it.

"I heard about Ginger. I'm sorry," Ellen said as she looked up from where she was mixing something in a bowl.

"Thanks."

"I just sold my last puppy yesterday from my latest litter, and I won't have any more until next year. Or I would have offered her to you. She was...the best of the bunch, and I was going to keep her for myself, but the person who bought her was very persuasive." She smiled. "They were desperate for a dog."

"Yeah. On one hand, I want to go out today and get another dog, because...I just love having one by my side all the time. It makes life a lot more interesting. But on the other, I don't know if I'll ever be able to get another dog who could live up to Ginger. She was pretty special."

"I know what you mean. Chewy's been with me forever, and she's getting older as well. It's...going to be hard when she goes. But I keep loving her anyway, even though I know the parting is going to be gut wrenching."

"Yeah. That's a really great word. It totally describes the way I feel."

Alaska came over and put an arm around Claudia. Claudia leaned into her.

"I know that you're going to be busy, and later today you have your first musical ensemble practice, but I was wondering if you might be interested in delivering this to Agathe after you're done practicing? I can't go today because Ezra and I are taking the children to the circus in Rockerton."

"Of course. I'd love to. Do I need to cook it too?" Claudia didn't feel like going to visit anyone, and she definitely didn't feel like even having a musical practice, but she did want to stay busy, and she was happy that she could help Alaska and Ezra. Their relationship was new, and it couldn't be easy trying to develop a bond with two children underfoot all the time.

Alaska gave her directions, and Claudia agreed to do it. It would give her something to keep her busy this evening.

"She wanted to have it so that she could feed her husband before she went to her support group meeting. She's never been to one before, and she's a little nervous."

"I'm sure it's going to go well for her. And I'm glad that she has other people to lean on. It must be very difficult to try to take care of your husband when...he's fading like that." Not only did she wonder about how her body might break down, but she wondered about her brain too. Ginger hadn't seemed to have any cognitive decline, but dogs were different than people, of course.

At any rate, if she did, she would appreciate people gathering around and helping her, so she was happy that she would be able to do that little thing for Agathe. Of course, she needed to get through their first musical practice. A shot of excitement ran through her when she remembered, she had the money and she could order the music.

Although, she needed to wait and see who showed up, to see what exactly she should get. Surely there would be people of different levels of ability and interest, different instruments, and she wanted to make things fun for the musicians, as well as for their audience when they played.

Getting her mind off of Ginger would be the best thing, and so she set to work helping the ladies put breakfast on the table and threw herself into the work for the day. Reminding her siblings that she needed to quit early so she could get ready for practice.

Maybe, maybe she would give Ellen a call later and see if she could reserve a puppy from her next litter. As much as she would like to have one now, she figured the Lord had worked it out so that the one puppy wasn't available, and she would have some time to mourn her loss.

The thought of a new puppy made her smile almost as much as her thoughts of the flowers. And she thought Ginger would approve.

Chapter Seven

Claudia looked at her phone. 4:05 p.m. Great. She tried to put a positive spin on the situation, but her heart felt like it was lying at her feet.

Five people had shown up for her musical ensemble, and four of them were elementary school kids who were probably there because their parents made them.

She had one high school student who played the flute and loved it. Claudia had talked to Sherie multiple times, since Sherie was considering a career in music and knew that Claudia had a degree.

Not that it made her any better or smarter than anyone else. All she could tell Sherie was what college had taught her. She didn't have any real-life experience.

And that was one of the things she had been sure to emphasize—it was extremely difficult to make a living from a person's art. It was possible, but difficult.

Music was often something that a person did on the side, the same way a person might paint pictures or do any hobby on the side. She might make a little bit of money by giving lessons or playing for weddings, but the days of making a living as a musician were pretty much over. Unless of course she got a job teaching in a school, but even schools were shutting down their music programs.

It was a discouraging thought for Claudia, except she loved the ranch and was happy working on it.

Maybe this idea had been a bad one.

She took a breath and was about to welcome everyone when the back door opened and a dark figure walked in carrying a large case. Probably a horn player, from the size and shape of his case.

Her own viola would mesh nicely with the flute, but she could hardly play and direct at the same time.

The elementary school students represented the string section anyway, with three violins and a cello. The cello was almost as big as the little boy sitting in the chair behind it.

He had tape on the fingerboard, and she assumed that he must be a beginner.

At least the person walking in seemed to be an adult. But she hadn't turned the lights in the back of the basement on, using only what they needed in the corner where she'd set their chairs up.

She put a welcoming smile on her face and waited for the person to walk into the light so she could recognize them and greet them by name. The way she'd done with the other five players.

Except, her heart lodged in her throat and her temples throbbed as the person took several more steps forward and she realized who it was.

Beau Hansen. Carrying a French horn.

This could be a major disaster. He obviously saw her sign-up sheets around town and decided that he could crash her ensemble, bringing the loudest instrument he could possibly find, so that he could...ruin everything? Or make a joke out of it.

One of the two.

But she hadn't given him the benefit of the doubt the last time she'd seen him, and she had been wrong. She had even thought that the next time she saw him, she would owe him an apology.

That apology was the furthest thing from her mind as she tried to get her thoughts under control. She couldn't just assume that he was there to sabotage everything that she was working toward. And she couldn't assume that he wanted to laugh and make fun of her either. Well, she could, but it wasn't right. If he caused a disturbance or did something that was out of line, she would simply tell him that he needed to leave.

Of course, she wasn't going to be able to make him leave, but...God had given her brothers. All of her brothers liked Beau, and none of them would want to help her toss him out on his ear, but...maybe she could talk one of them into standing at the door for the next practice and keep him out.

Or, more likely, maybe she could get one of them to ask him to help them with something on the farm so he couldn't make the next practice. Or any other practice in the future.

Until he does something unkind, you be nice. And don't forget about your apology.

All right. Pep talk over. She pasted a smile on her face, which pinched like plastic, and said, "Oh! Welcome. I didn't realize you played the French horn."

"We didn't go to school together, but I played all through high school. I...was looking forward to today when I saw your ad hanging in the hardware store."

"All right, well, make yourself at home. We're just getting ready to start."

He nodded, and she pointed to one of the violin players.

"Can we tune your instrument so we can get the rest of the orchestra ensemble on pitch?" she asked, pulling out a tuning fork.

The little boy's brows puckered, but he nodded uncertainly as she slapped the fork against her leg and then held it out so she could put it on his instrument.

It made that beautiful "A" sound, and she said, "Now play your A string."

He did, and it sounded like it was at least half a step flat.

"All right, we need to tighten that up a little," she said.

The boy just looked at her. And then, silently, he handed his instrument over with a solemn expression, like he was offering it to her.

Tuning a violin wasn't much different than tuning her viola, and she took it carefully.

His pegs were so sticky and tight that they were difficult to move, and she ended up loosening them before she could get them tightened, plucking the strings near the fingerboard, since she didn't want the oil from her fingers to touch the part of the string where the bow went, to get them close in tune before she put it under her chin.

It took her a few minutes to get it dialed in, and she thought she probably should have started tuning instruments twenty minutes ago if she wanted to get started in a timely manner, if this was what she was going to have to do with everyone's instrument.

Glancing over, she saw that Beau had taken a chair, gotten his horn out of its case, put the mouthpiece on, and sat fingering the valves, ready to start.

He looked at her with interest, and as she glanced at his face, she didn't see any mockery there at all.

It was a good thing, because she felt rather emotionally fragile, and she wasn't sure she was up to their verbal sparring at the moment.

"All right. Ollie is going to play an A for us, and we're all going to tune our instruments to his. Okay?"

The kids had probably never been in a musical setting before, since Sweet Water Elementary did not have an orchestra, and possibly that was why their parents had brought them today. To get that experience. Well, she could adjust her expectations. This could become an experience for the kids, except...there was Beau. And of course Sherie.

She wasn't sure how they were all going to come together, but she would take what the Lord gave her and do her best with it.

She ended up tuning the cello as well, although the other two kids, to her surprise, were able to tune their own violins.

Beau had made a slight adjustment with his horn and then quit playing so that he didn't overshadow the other kids and they were able to hear their note.

Sherie had taken slightly longer to adjust her flute, but then she followed Beau's example and laid her instrument on her lap while the other younger kids worked on getting their strings in tune.

Claudia didn't think that she would ever say it, but she appreciated Beau's example.

"All right, string section," she said. "Your first assignment for next week is to learn to tune your own instrument. If you need to see me after lessons, I can help you with it, or you can discuss it with your teacher and your parents." She continued to talk for a short while, explaining the way an orchestra usually tuned itself.

There wasn't really much response on the faces of the kids who stared at her. A couple of them nodded, but most of them just gazed vacantly at her like they had no idea what she was saying.

Two of them had been able to tune their own instruments anyway, so she was really only talking to two of them, but she didn't want to single them out and embarrass them, so that's why she said "string section."

"All right, group. Today is about figuring out where we're at and what kind of music we need to get. So we're going to start out with a few scales. Can everyone play a C scale?" She looked around and then realized that was probably not the best question to ask.

"If you cannot play a C scale, would you please raise your hand or your bow?" She smiled at the string players.

One bow went up.

All right. She took a breath. She could do this.

It was going to be harder than she thought, and it was going to look differently than what she had planned, but...she really thought this was a door that the Lord was opening, and if this was what He was going to have it look like, this was how she was going to roll with it.

She tried to keep that attitude throughout the next forty-five minutes as she had the people who were able to play scales and then asked them about their favorite music, trying to get a feel for what level they're playing at. One of the string players surprised her and was better than she thought.

She would move that little girl to first chair, and she probably would be wise to just keep them all in the same section, rather than trying to have first violins and second violins. As much as she would like to do that. Maybe, if they stuck with it, she would eventually get to the point where she wanted to be.

This is a good starting place, she told herself as she thanked everyone for coming and told them to be sure to grab some refreshments afterward. She'd baked cookies and brought juice. Way too much, but she hadn't known how many people were coming, and she wanted to make sure that she had enough for everyone.

Whatever was left, her brothers would eat it up fast. They never had a problem getting rid of food at her house.

She smiled at each person as they came up to grab some cookies. And she tried to ignore the fact that Beau had put his horn away but had not left. He stood in the back for a couple of minutes, talking to Sherie, and then he said a couple of words to each of the string players as they munched on their cookies and filed out of the church.

Finally, it was just Claudia and him in the basement. Which made Claudia itchy. She didn't like to be alone with him.

"Where's Mina?" he asked as he came up to the table and looked over the cookies.

"She's at home. I'm delivering a casserole to Agathe after I'm done here, and she's making sure that it's in the oven at the right time and comes out when it's done."

She felt like an idiot. She didn't have to explain every little thing that Mina was doing.

"I'm sorry about Ginger." His voice held compassion and was pitched low, and he sounded sincere, like he really was sorry.

Except... How did he even know?

And then she remembered it was a small town. Ginger had passed yesterday, and so only the people who were really out of the loop wouldn't know.

"Yeah. Me too." She pressed her lips together. "Thanks."

He nodded, biting into a cookie. He chewed for a bit, and then he said, "Did you make these?"

"Yeah. I guess I could've cut it down by about half. I...had hoped that more people would show up."

She told herself to close her mouth. She didn't want to unload her troubles and burdens onto him. Beau was the last person she wanted to talk about that stuff with.

Except she did owe him something.

"Maybe more people will come next week. Sorry I was late. I'll try to be on time next time."

"You're coming back?" she said before she could stop herself. She assumed that he had come just to make fun of her, and maybe out of pity, because he saw how pathetic everything was, with only five kids showing up, he decided that she did a good enough job of making herself look like an idiot, and she didn't need his help.

"Sure. I...kinda miss playing in the band. It was nice to dust off the old horn and get it out for a bit."

"You're quite good, actually," she said, and she tried not to be reluctant with her praise. It was true. He really was good.

"It seemed to come naturally to me. Once I was able to read music, it wasn't hard to learn to play at all. Although, horns don't usually have a very interesting part. It's often basically percussion notes."

"Yeah. Sorry about that." And then she brightened. "If you're really going to stick around, we can find some music that features the horn."

"Of course I'm going to stick around. I told you. I enjoy it."

She lifted her shoulder and didn't say anything. Obviously, he was one of the few. And she also didn't exactly trust him. But she did need to get this apology out of her mouth before she never apologized.

"I owe you an apology. The latch on the endgate was broken. I accused you of opening that on purpose, but it wasn't your fault."

He looked surprised, and then the word rolled out of his mouth. "Thanks."

She looked down at the cookies, not knowing what else to say. She didn't really have anything to talk to him about, and just because he'd shown up today didn't mean that they were friends. In fact, she probably ought to continue to be suspicious.

Except she really wasn't the suspicious type. She was more like a trusting type, which was saying something, considering she had six brothers, and they all loved to tease her. She probably should be the most suspicious person on the planet, but they'd always made fun of her because she was so gullible. She just liked to believe people. She liked to be able to trust them. She hated not thinking the best about people, and that was kind of the way she was with Beau. She'd just assumed the worst about him.

"You know. I owe you an apology too. I... I got off to a bad start with you. I somehow got in the habit of teasing you and making fun of you every time we met, which feels very junior high to me, but it just seemed to be the stuff that kept coming out of my mouth, even though part of me was standing back in horror, unable to believe that I had been so unkind. Will you forgive me?"

His apology was much better than hers, if anyone was keeping track. She wished she had managed to apologize so nicely.

Then she remembered what she had just thought about her being gullible. Was this another one of those things? Where she was going to wish that she had thought it through and been a little suspicious?

"Of course I forgive you. I've been just as bad. Maybe even worse, and I'm usually not like that. I'm usually...a lot more trusting. And friendly."

"I know. I've noticed that that's the way you treat everyone else, except for me. And I realized that it was my fault that you didn't treat me like that because I had treated you badly. Can we...start over?" He held out his hand. She looked down at it, and then he said, "And I'm not just saying this because you make the best cookies I've ever eaten."

"I could tell your mom that, and she might not be very happy with you," she said as she grasped his hand and shook it.

"I think my mom would admit that she's the world's worst baker. I'm pretty sure my dad makes better cookies than she does. And that's not saying much."

"But your mom is beautiful. And kind and sweet. And that beats good cookies any day."

"Well, I can't argue with you on any of those fronts. My mom is pretty awesome."

How could she resist a man who loved his mother? Of course, Mrs. Hansen was everything he'd said, and even more. Still, she really appreciated the fact that he respected her. And she suspected that he would, even if she wasn't as good as what she was. Of course, that was just conjecture on her part, and she could be wrong.

She smiled at him, unsure what else to say. Just because they talked to each other and issued apologies didn't make them friends.

"Well, I guess I'll see you around. Tomorrow in church... Unless you're going to continue to run from me?"

He noticed? She wanted to sink through the floor, and she felt like an idiot.

"Sorry. I don't seem to be able to keep a decent tongue in my head when you are around, and I figured that the church was not the place for me to be unkind to you. I... Yeah. I'll try not to run if I see you in church. Anymore," she added.

He had a little smile on his face, but his eyes were hooded and maybe a bit sad. Like he knew that she was justified in what she just said, because he hadn't been kind.

"Good point." He tilted his head a bit and then said, "A couple of my cousins play instruments as well. Maybe I can get them to come. I'm guessing today didn't turn out quite the way you wanted it to."

"No. I had a lot bigger plans and higher hopes, but this is what God gave me to work with, so this is what I'm going to use to start. And...I'm not going to let it get me down."

"That's the spirit. I like it." He grinned. "I'll see what my cousins say. Two of them play the violin, and I know a couple horn players."

"Well. They're all welcome. Although, I'm sure they've seen the signs in town. I had them up for a month."

"Yeah. Spring's a busy season for ranchers, and I know they're busy, but it never hurts to take time off and have a little fun." He grinned. "And good food helps."

"Take a handful for the road. Otherwise, my brothers are going to eat them."

"All right. I'll do it."

He paused, as though he was going to say something else, and then he waved his handful of cookies in the air. "See ya around."

She nodded. "Yeah. See you around."

He couldn't possibly see her, and she didn't really think about it as her eyes lingered on him as he walked back into the darkness and out the door. Carrying his horn, like it wasn't nearly as heavy as she knew it to be.

Today had not gone as she planned, not even a little. But she wasn't unhappy. Interesting how the Lord worked things out. They might not go according to plan, but they went according to His plan, which, she had to admit, was always better.

Chapter Eight

Agathe opened her door and smiled at the young woman and the little girl in front of her.

"Oh my goodness. Do come in!" she said, holding the door open. Jim had been having a very good day and had known who she was almost the entire day.

It always made her heart happy when she got one more day to spend with him.

She supposed that showed on her face as she welcomed her guests, who had brought supper for her.

She was a little nervous about going to the support group. It wasn't necessarily meeting the other people, although she had always been more of an introvert. But it was more about admitting that she was truly doing this. That her husband was fading away, that Alzheimer's was changing their lives, and that she needed help.

"Oh, that smells so good!" she said as Claudia walked in. "I don't think I've met your friend, Claudia." She closed the door behind them, and Claudia, who had been there a few times, carried the casserole dish to the kitchen, leading the way.

"That's Mina. She's staying with me for the summer. Mina, this is Agathe. And somewhere around here is her husband, Mr. Jim."

"Nice to meet you, Miss Agathe," Mina said respectfully.

Agathe liked the look of the little girl. She had sparkling eyes and looked like she was one of those kids who was perpetually happy and enjoyed a good joke. Agathe had been more reserved as a child, but she had friends like this little girl, Mina, and she could relate to her.

"It's good to meet you too. I love that you're helping Claudia. She is always into something, and she needs a good helper."

"I'm having a lot of fun on the ranch. It's a lot different than where I lived in Wyoming."

"North Dakota is definitely one of a kind, and life on the ranch is never boring from what I understand," she said.

"We have some company, I see," Jim said as he walked into the kitchen.

"Jim, darling, you remember Claudia, and this is her new friend, Mina."

"I always love anyone who brings me food," Jim said, his old charm coming to the forefront. She had been quiet and subdued. He had been the one who had been the charmer, the outgoing, vivacious, always trying to get her to do something that was just a little bit outside of her comfort zone kind of guy. Of course, moving to America was a lot outside of her comfort zone, but the years she spent with Jim had been totally worth it.

She supposed their planned trip back to her childhood country would never come to fruition, but she could dream.

She chatted for a bit, but Claudia was never one to stand around, and she had things to do, so she and Mina left. Of course, they knew she was on her way to her support group meeting.

Although she took time to eat with her husband first and left him sitting in front of the TV set, with the sports channel on. He should be just fine for a few hours; in fact, he would probably fall asleep in front of it.

Taking a light jacket, because the temperatures would likely be pretty chilly by the time she returned, she got in her car and drove to the Olympic training center, where they were meeting in the boardroom.

Part of the stipulations for building the center was that they would open their building for the town, whenever it wasn't in use for sports-related activities.

The training center had been more than wonderful about it, and beyond the Alzheimer's support group, Agathe had enjoyed her aquatics class, and before that, she and Jim had played couples tennis for years.

Of course, they were both beyond that, although she might take up walking. She understood that the training center was rather large, and a group met to walk around it to do laps inside in the winter.

Jim wasn't even that bad yet, according to what she'd heard, but sometimes she just longed to get out. But going anywhere with him became more and more difficult because she didn't know when he would suddenly have no idea of who she was, or where they were, or get upset, accusing her of kidnapping him and taking her away from…she didn't even know what. Since she was his family.

The room was brightly lit, and there were eight to ten other people already there. There was one empty chair in the circle, and she felt a little conspicuous as she sat down in it. A sober-looking woman sat on her left, but on her right, a man glanced at her and smiled.

He had bright blue eyes that reminded her of Jim's. And she found herself smiling back.

Throughout her marriage, she never really paid much attention to men. One man was enough for her, and she had focused all of her attention and adoration on him. Maybe she just longed for a little affection or friendship or something.

She missed the deep conversations she and Jim used to have, but even more, she missed the little touches and the affection that used to flow between them. Now, he was just as likely to push her away, and it hurt her more than she wanted to admit. Until she sat down in that chair and looked into that stranger's eyes, she hadn't realized that perhaps she was vulnerable to something she had never been vulnerable to in her life before. And that was looking at a man who wasn't her husband.

She jerked her eyes away and fiddled with her purse that she set in her lap, and then decided to put it underneath her chair. She unzipped her jacket but didn't take it off, not wanting to risk bumping either of the two people who were seated next to her. She wasn't very comfortable in a circle of people. It...seemed a little too intimate, and these were all strangers.

"Welcome, class. I see we have a new member today, so, I don't want to embarrass you, but the rest of us all know each other, and we want to know you too. We are all dealing with loved ones who are in various stages of Alzheimer's, and I'm guessing that's why you're here. Since we're the Alzheimer's support group. I am Freda Stone, and I'm from Rockerton. So I'm sorry if everyone else knows you, and I'm just out of the loop because I'm not from your small town."

There was silence, and Agathe figured it was probably her turn to speak. As soon as she opened her mouth, people would be able to tell by her accent that she wasn't a native American.

She had gotten used to that over the years and found Americans very accepting of people who were from a different culture. Sometimes she felt a little out of the loop, because there were people who'd lived in the same area for generations, but that was true in France as well. Although, from what she understood, that was changing, but when she grew up, she had known people who had been in the same area for a hundred years if not far more.

"I'm Agathe. And I do know most of you. A few faces are unfamiliar," she said, not daring to look at the man beside her again. That first look, where she felt the pull and a longing that was both familiar and completely out of character, had been enough for her to know that she needed to be careful.

Or maybe, it was okay. That was what she was here for. Not to hook up with anyone, of course, but because she was losing something that she valued and loved, and so was he. They would...have things in common. Yes.

As she continued to talk, she allowed her eyes to drift over to the man, who listened intently as she spoke.

"I've lived in Sweet Water all of my married life, as my husband was from here originally. We met in France, when he was in the service. He was handsome and dashing and..." To her horror, tears filled her eyes, and she paused to breathe and push them back before she continued. "Now, sometimes...he doesn't know who I am. And we don't go out nearly like we used to, because he'll forget where we are, and accuse me of kidnapping him, and—"

She stopped abruptly. She was only supposed to introduce herself, not give her life story and start pouring out all of her troubles.

"I'm sorry. I guess that's enough about me."

"No. Don't apologize. That's what we're here for. We're here because all of us are feeling that to some extent. And it's helpful to know that we're not the only ones. I... I love my mother and my dad, and they both had Alzheimer's for years before they passed. I took care of them both in my home, and I'm quite familiar with the disease. It's a terrible one, and what you're feeling is exactly the same way so many of us felt. Although I understand it's different to lose a parent than it is to lose a husband." The woman sounded very benevolent and understanding, and Agathe appreciated her kindness.

"Now, Agathe might look familiar to most of us, but she's not familiar with everyone, so we'll go around the circle, and everyone will say as much as you are comfortable with. Remember, just as someone else's story helps you, your story can help them. So don't be afraid to say whatever's on your mind, or whatever you are struggling with, or whatever positive thing you have to say is welcome as well." She looked to her right. "Blanche, we'll start with you."

Agathe listened as they went through the first four or five in the circle. Some of them talked a little bit, some longer than others, about what they were going through. She found herself excited and eagerly anticipating what the man beside her would say.

Finally, it was his turn, and she watched him with the same interest with which he had listened to her.

"My name is Waylen." He looked at her, nodding with sincerity. "It's nice to meet you, Agathe. You remind me a little of my wife. She passed away three months ago. She had Alzheimer's for ten years. And I cared for her through all but the last year and a half. It had just gotten to be...too much."

His voice trailed off a little, and Agathe's heart went out to him.

"Anyway. Eight hard years of caring for someone with Alzheimer's, and I feel like I really don't know anything at all. Other than it's lonely, and it's hard, watching the person you love slowly stop recognizing you, until you're always a stranger. My wife remained sweet and kind until the very last days, although I understand some people's personalities change. Anyway, it was hard, and I miss her, and I was lonely, which is why I joined this group."

Agathe was speechless when he was done. He had cared for his wife for eight years! Jim had only been on the journey for maybe two. He'd been diagnosed a little over a year prior, and maybe he had been slowly fading before that. She didn't think she could handle another eight years of it. But he was otherwise healthy, had always been in great shape, and his body could well outlast his mind, for decades even.

She almost cringed at the thought. Did she have the fortitude to stay with her husband even if he didn't know who she was? Could she care for him that long? It had only been a little over a year, and already she was lonely and longed for a gentle hand on her shoulder, strong arms to hold her, and a chest to lean her head on. All of those things that her husband had provided over the years but now did not.

That's the way the meeting went, with multiple people talking about how they felt, and Freda facilitating the meeting while not being overbearing. She didn't tell them what to do, but she did have some advice and pointers, and they ended the meeting with Agathe not feeling encouraged exactly, but feeling like she met people who were going through the exact same thing she was and that they understood.

She was a little bit discouraged, because she understood from the meeting that her journey had just begun. She was looking down a long, dark road, one that potentially could be one of the hardest things she'd ever done. Already, she had struggled, and there were a lot more struggles to come. She could see that clearly now.

But she wasn't alone, and that was where the value of the group came in. These other people had been through it or were going through it now. Waylen was on the other side. That was an encouragement too. That there would be hope and light at the end of this.

Although, there had been a couple of hints of people who had not fared so well. One lady who had passed away while caring for her husband. And her husband had been put in a home. Another lady who had gotten sick and who had not been able to care for her husband anymore.

Still, all in all, the meeting had been an encouragement, and she knew as she gathered up her purse and zipped her jacket that she would be returning.

The lady on her left spoke a few words to her before she moved between the chairs and hurried out, skipping the refreshments that were offered on the back table.

"The cookies are usually really good," Waylen said from her right side. She hadn't realized he'd followed her out. He would have almost had to run.

"Oh. Good to know. I guess I'll try one then."

"I wondered if you like cookies. You...seem like a woman who maybe doesn't."

He didn't say anything more, and she wasn't sure whether he was commenting on her figure, her accent, or just putting a comment out into the universe.

"I have a terrible sweet tooth, but I've tried not to indulge it too much over the years. I figured that my husband would prefer that I tried to stay as trim as possible. Not that he only loved me because of the way I looked." Her voice trailed off a little, because the idea made her sad. Jim would have loved her no matter how she looked, but she knew that he would most likely be happier if she were physically healthy, and everything that she'd read about men indicated that they preferred to have a nice figure to look at. She didn't know how accurate that was, and Jim would never say, but it was healthy and good for her anyway, so she did it for them both.

"I would say Jim's a lucky man, then," Waylen said, and there was a bit of sadness in his eyes. "I'm glad you came today. I hope the meeting was informative to you. I wish I would have had a group like this when I was going through what I did with my wife."

"Yeah. I... I guess I have mixed feelings about it. While I am encouraged, because there are other people going through the same thing, it's a little discouraging to know how long it can last. You said you spent eight and a half years taking care of your wife. I've only been in this a little over a year, and I'm exhausted. I don't know if I can go eight and a half."

"No. It's better if you just look at today. If you start trying to look at the big picture, it becomes almost unbearable."

"I've always been a big-picture person. Although, I do love to watch the grass grow, and watch ladybugs, or see the minute details of nature. Still, in my life, I've always been big picture."

"I like to know the end before the beginning. But I guess that's what got me through those years with my wife. I... I had to look at it day by day. Because when I tried to do what I wanted to do, which was try to figure out how much longer it was going to last and how I was ever going to survive, I got depressed. And you can't be a good caretaker when you're dealing with your own depression."

She was surprised that a man like him would admit to depression. She...couldn't imagine Jim saying that he was depressed. He just seemed too...manly for that, she supposed. She liked Waylen's honesty, the fact that he wasn't pulling any punches, and he could admit that he wasn't perfect. That in itself took a certain type of strength, one she admired.

"All right. You're right about the cookies by the way." She held up the one that she'd taken two bites out of while he was talking. "I better get back home. I left Jim in front of the TV watching sports, and while he usually doesn't move and will probably be asleep... I just can't say for sure."

Waylen nodded, like he understood completely.

"I usually had someone watch her if I needed to go out." He paused. "I'm retired, although I have a couple of things I do on the side. But if you need to go out, I can come and stay with him if you want me to."

Her eyes grew big. She hadn't imagined that. She hated to ask any of her lady friends, because Jim could be...very strong when he wanted to be, and while she didn't expect him to manhandle anyone, he had done some things that were completely out of character, and she really didn't want to subject any of her friends to any of his unexpected, and potentially even dangerous, actions.

"Would you really?"

He nodded. "I've been there, remember?"

"All right. Maybe I'll take you up on that." Then she realized she could hardly take him up on it when she had no way of contacting him. But she hesitated, remembering the thought that she had when she sat down. She was vulnerable. And she'd never gotten a man's number who wasn't her husband in her entire life before. She just hadn't gone there.

But this was a support group. He was here to support her. He was *offering* to support her, and she would be silly to not take him up on that, right?

"Can I have your number?" she asked, just as calmly as she could. She...had never said that to a man before.

"Sure. Actually, give me yours and I'll send you a text." He had his phone out, with his fingers poised above it, waiting, and she rattled off her number.

He sent her a text immediately, and her phone buzzed in her pocket.

"I'll see you around. Next week, if not before."

She nodded. "I'll definitely be back."

She pulled her phone out of her pocket so that she could put his contact information in as she walked out of the training center.

She smiled when she saw what he had texted her, recognizing the quote but realizing she hadn't seen it for a while.

Every storm runs out of rain.

Chapter Nine

"You guys can just be happy that you didn't play instruments in school. Or Beau would have you roped into doing this music ensemble as well," Gordon said as he stood with Beau and their other cousins, Merle and Marshall.

"I did not rope you into anything. You want to. Admit it."

"When you said cookies, I felt myself weakening, but to say that I wanted to, that might be a slight exaggeration."

"All right. But cookies are cookies, and you know you were just looking for an opportunity to play the trumpet again."

"Actually...okay. I don't exactly miss it, but an hour a week is worth the sacrifice, especially if it helps you finally find someone who can put up with you long enough for you to get a ring on her finger."

The other guys laughed, and Beau smiled, but he didn't see the humor in that as much as everyone else. He wasn't looking for a woman who would put up with him. He wanted a woman who would look at him the way his mom looked at his dad.

He wanted a woman who would not be able to walk by him without reaching out to touch him, who would sit as close as she could to him when they were on the porch swing at night, and who would always see the best in him, no matter what he did.

Yeah, probably his mom was one in a million, but he was hoping he found someone like her.

He saw Claudia in his mind's eye, and he again wondered if God's timing was part of what was going on. He just knew that he had never been this interested in a woman before, but he also knew that he had a tendency to extrapolate what he wanted and call it God's will. He didn't want to make a mistake of that magnitude and end up married to her. But at the same time, he didn't want to miss out either. Because he thought Claudia could be, if not perfect, at least someone who would be able to put up with him, as his cousin suggested.

"Your parents should have had you in some kind of musical situation, considering how much you like to tap on anything you can get your hands on." Marshall smirked at Merle. "I don't remember how many times you got in trouble in class for tapping on someone's head with your pencil."

"I have no idea why they didn't have me playing the drums somewhere."

"I think when you become a parent, you'll have a much better idea of why they didn't send you off to play the drums." Beau didn't have any trouble figuring it out now. He would definitely encourage his children to play the quietest instrument possible. Was there an instrument that made no sound?

He didn't know how his parents put up with him practicing the French horn, which he had done almost nonstop for an entire year. He learned more in that year than he learned the rest of the time he played the instrument in school, but it had been good, since it had laid a good foundation for him as his interest waned.

He still found it something interesting to do on snowy North Dakota nights when the temperature was too cold to even think about going outside unless there was some kind of emergency with his animals.

Gordon had already agreed to go, and he didn't seem like it was going to be a hardship. Beau had also asked his cousins Ophie and Zelma, and they had agreed as well. They had all been together in the band in high school, even though Zelma had played the cello. There hadn't been any other place for her, so they'd made a place for it in the band. She didn't march at football games, but that was probably just as well, since she had ended up being a cheerleader.

"There she is. Are you going to go over and see if she runs from you again?" Merle gave a knowing look to Beau, and Beau wondered just how transparent he'd been. Of course, his cousins knew him better than anyone, since they'd grown up together, and they were almost like brothers. He had older sisters growing up and appreciated the times he'd gotten to spend with his cousins.

As much as he loved his sisters.

Beau watched Claudia from under his brows as she joined a group of teenage girls and chatted with them for a bit. Church was filling up, and he probably should go sit where he'd left his Bible in the pew. He knew Claudia most likely was going downstairs to be in the nursery. But instead of doing what he knew he should, he left his cousins, without even saying goodbye, and walked toward her.

He hadn't been able to approach her in church for years, if ever, and he wouldn't have been surprised if she looked up to see him coming and moved away immediately.

Instead, she looked up, saw him, and while she didn't quite smile, there might have been a little bit of humor in her eyes, responding to the grin that was on his own face. It was like they were having a little conversation above the chatter of everyone else. He might have been asking, "Remember what we said yesterday? Are you going to stay?"

And she might have been saying, "I told you I would."

The girls moved away, and Claudia stood in front of him.

"Hello," he said, feeling like a dork for not being able to think of anything else to say. He could tease her about letting him capture her or some such other thing, but that was what had gotten him in trouble to begin with. He had been teasing her, and it had turned...not exactly nasty, but he had unintentionally pushed her too far.

He wanted to be careful not to do that again. Maybe he had tried to tease her before they knew each other well enough for her to know that he didn't mean anything by it.

Or...maybe there was something else. She grew up with six brothers though, so he knew she had to be used to being teased.

"Hey. I didn't run."

"I see that. I...feel honored."

"I bet you do."

"I figured you were on your way to the nursery. So, I guess I wouldn't have been totally upset if you had hurried off."

"Actually, it's not my week. And someone's already sitting in my usual seat, so I figured I'd wait until things settle down and slip in with one of my siblings."

"There's a spot right here where I set my Bible. You can sit with me if you want to."

She gave two big blinks, and he wished he would have kept his mouth shut. There definitely was room in the pew where he laid his Bible earlier, but it was never a good idea for friends to sit together in church. Rumors always swirled about them becoming more. And he wasn't even sure if Claudia was his friend.

"Are we good enough friends to sit together in church?" he asked, figuring there was no point in sitting around wondering about it.

"I don't think we're that good of friends," she said, and he didn't take offense, because she was laughing. "Unless of course, we want everyone to be planning our wedding this afternoon."

"I think you'd make a beautiful bride, and I could see you wearing a nontraditional dress. Maybe a green one. One to match your eyes. And not in the traditional wedding gown shape. Maybe more like a sundress. You'd have a straw hat, and you would carry a bouquet of daisies. I'll be in jeans and a T-shirt, and you'll be happy that they're clean and not care that I didn't get dressed up."

"I think you'd look good in a suit. In fact, I'm gonna hold out for a suit."

"Yesterday she wouldn't talk to me, today she's planning my wedding."

Her mouth opened in an O, her eyes got wide, and she put her hands on her hips. "That was not me!"

"You just said you want me to wear a suit to our wedding. Did I mishear you?"

"Yes! I mean, no, I mean...you are terrible."

"I know. I'm sorry. I guess I shouldn't have grown up with sisters. If

I had brothers, they'd have made fun of me all the time, and I probably would be more compassionate or something."

She laughed a little, and he wasn't sure exactly what he said that was so funny. But he couldn't deny that he enjoyed listening to her laugh.

"So, are you going to live on the wild side, or do you prefer to stay single for a while longer, at least in the eyes of your church family?"

"I really don't enjoy living on the wild side. I definitely like seatbelts and safety harnesses."

"And hard hats. You'd look cute in a hard hat."

"Thank you. To match your suit. And my wedding dress."

"Well... I guess I could honestly say I have never been to a wedding where the bride-to-be wore a hard hat. Ours is going to be unique anyway."

"It would be green to match my dress. And your tie. Definitely your tie needs to match the hard hat. I'm pretty sure that's in the wedding etiquette book."

"I must have missed that page."

"You read it! Okay, that's the thing I'm going to share with people."

He laughed. "You share away and see if they believe you."

"True. I probably ought to have you say it again so I can videotape it. I need evidence for this."

"That's fine, you get your phone out and videotape me saying that, and I'll get mine out and videotape you saying your hard hat is going to be green at your wedding."

"Deal. But I'm not sure I'm going to be able to find all that in a bridal shop."

"You'll be the only woman you know who went shopping for your wedding in a hardware store."

"Oh, is that where you get hard hats?"

"I'm not sure. You'll probably find safety goggles there though. Do they need to match the hard hats?"

"Yours or mine?" she asked, and somehow, they had started moving toward his seat. He couldn't stop the stirring hope, because he was pretty sure she was going to sit with him after all.

"We both should wear them. After all, that'll be a little bit of a nod to the way our relationship started out, right?"

"It was so terrible we needed to wear protective gear when we were around each other? People are really going to wonder about our wedding night."

Whoa. He wasn't going to go there. But she did, so...was it okay for him to?

"I would have to draw the line at the video camera on our honeymoon. Not in the bedroom anyway."

Her cheeks had gotten pink, which was cute, but she seemed to understand that they were doing it in fun, and she didn't look upset as she slid into the pew where his Bible already sat.

He wanted to do a fist pump, but he consoled himself with a smile instead. She was sitting beside him, voluntarily, and not running away, and was talking to him. If he would have known that spending one hour at her ensemble practice was going to yield this big of results, he would have encouraged her to start one years ago.

Of course, her family hadn't been in Sweet Water that long, but...it was for the best. He hadn't been ready to court a girl before that. It was funny how perfect God's timing could be.

"We have so many things in common, we're practically twins."

"We do?" she said, her brows furrowing as he sat down.

"Sure. We both love safety glasses and hard hats, you agreed to green, which happens to be my favorite color, and we both agree that we don't want any video cameras in the bedroom. I really can't think of too much else that we could possibly be the same in."

"I know we definitely disagree about you in the suit. The T-shirt is not acceptable."

"You're in a sundress. Why can't I be in a T-shirt?"

"You put me in a sundress. If I choose, I'm definitely choosing a wedding gown. A big one, the biggest I can find, with the train that stretches the whole way down the aisle and goes out the door. Along with a veil. The veil has to be long and frilly and so fluffy I won't even be able to see as I make my way down the aisle. After all, if you're scared to death, it's best to close your eyes. If I have a veil on that big, no one will be able to tell that my eyes are tightly shut."

"You're scared? Why are you so scared? Is it the safety goggles? I can take them off."

She laughed. "No. The idea of spending the rest of my life with someone...what if I made a mistake? What if I choose the wrong person? What if I'm stuck? That's... That's an awful long time to be stuck with someone who wasn't the right person."

He was quiet for a bit. Maybe she didn't realize it, but what she said showed a lot about her character. She wasn't saying *what if I have to go through a divorce?* She was saying whether she was stuck...in other words, if she made a mistake and married someone who turned out to be not what she thought he was, she was thinking she was going to be stuck with him. She was going to stay.

She was going to keep her vows.

That probably did more to make him feel like she was exactly what he thought she was than anything else she said, although he did appreciate a woman with a sense of humor. And he had enjoyed bantering with her more than he enjoyed talking with his cousins, which was saying something. In fact, he realized that he'd rather spend time with her than them and was trying to figure out in the back of his mind how he could finagle a date or something.

He told himself to slow down. To relax. That there was time. He didn't have to ask her out the very first day she actually started talking to him. He could give her time to...warm up to him a little, for her to decide she liked him as much as he liked her. Of course, it was a nice first step that she'd sat down on his pew with him. He still wasn't sure why.

Regardless, the pastor started service, and they both faced forward, effectively ending the conversation. Although, it didn't keep Beau from smiling.

He saw his mom glance back once, her eyes widening, and then she elbowed his dad. It took his dad a little while, as he shifted, his arm already around his wife, and he turned his head, ostensibly scratching his chin.

The disfigurement on his dad's face had maybe gotten worse through the years as he'd aged, but people who knew him didn't notice it at all. And for as long as Beau had known him, his dad had not been self-conscious about it. His mom had mentioned a few times that it used to really bother his dad, but maybe it was the love of his mom that had brought him out of whatever prison it was that made him think that his looks were all he had.

Regardless, people often remarked to Beau that with the genetics that he had, it was inevitable that he would be handsome.

His parents both cautioned him about thinking too much about it. Warning him that it was what was inside that really counted, and emphasizing that not just for himself but for any girl he might be interested in.

He was pretty sure Claudia fit the bill, but she was pretty as well. Beautiful to him, but he wasn't used to going around and judging how women looked. He just knew that when he looked at her, he didn't want to stop.

Regardless, when his dad turned around, Beau was ready, and he raised his brows in his best imitation of the parental, "what are you doing looking behind you and not paying attention to the sermon in church?" look.

He thought it was rather effective, even if his dad did start to grin as he turned his head back around.

His dad leaned over, and Beau would have given a lot of money to know exactly what in the world his dad would have to say to his mom. His mom nodded, and he could tell she was smiling as she lifted her face and whispered back in his dad's ear.

He loved watching his parents. It made him feel secure first of all, because it was so obvious that they loved each other. But it also just did something to his soul. Just to see...maybe it was evidence that a marriage really could be a good thing. Where two people loved and respected each other.

And that it wasn't just a pipe dream on his part.

Regardless, the exchange made him smile, although his attention was caught by the sermon, and he stopped thinking about affection and marriages and parents, and while he didn't exactly stop thinking about Claudia, he did try to see what he could learn and apply to his life.

Chapter Ten

Claudia sat beside Beau Hansen. In church!

She almost giggled to herself. They'd been having a conversation that was fun. She could hardly believe it. She would have called him her enemy, even as recently as yesterday, but he'd shown up at her ensemble practice, and now, she was sitting beside him in church.

And she had to admit that he was probably the most handsome man she'd ever met. That was almost off putting to her though. She seemed to have learned that a lot of times when men were handsome, they were also conceited and lacked character, because they'd never had to develop any. Their looks had gotten them everything they had, which she assumed was probably true for women as well. Not that every beautiful woman that she knew was a terrible person, far from it. It just seemed to be a general rule and especially applicable to men.

But she had been pleasantly surprised with Beau. And she found herself looking forward to talking to him after the service was over. Which was kind of unbelievable.

Plus, he'd gone out of his way to make sure she knew he was helping her find people for her ensemble, which she found incredibly considerate. Especially since he probably really didn't give a flip about it. Other than...for her. That also was kind of crazy.

The pastor had a great message about putting God first and removing idols from her life, though she had a little bit of trouble concentrating because every time she looked down at her Bible, she could see Beau's jean-clad leg beside her, and her eyes just wanted to drift over and apparently enjoy the sight of him beside her.

Regardless, while she did get a little bit of something out of the message, she was not disappointed when it was over. Mostly because she was eager to talk to Beau a little bit more.

"Good message," he said as the closing prayer ended and the pianist began the postlude.

"Yeah. Very convicting," she said, and it was true. She had a tendency to forget that God was supposed to be the most important thing in her life, and she allowed the cares of the world to push in. Like with Ginger. She had been consumed with her dog dying, and while she had thought of heaven, she wondered if someone had told her that she wasn't allowed to go to church whether she'd have been quite so devastated.

She hardly thought so.

"So, do you have plans for the afternoon?" Beau asked as they shifted out of their pew and joined the line heading toward the back of the church, where the pastor greeted folks before they walked out the door.

"I have some things to do on the ranch, although we try to take it easy on Sundays."

"We do too." He paused and looked to the side.

She recognized his cousins, at least she was pretty sure they were his cousins, coming over. Having not grown up in Sweet Water, she was a little bit behind when it came to knowing who was related to who, but considering that two of them had the same last name as he did, she assumed that they were cousins.

"I had some ideas about your ensemble, but it looks like my cousins are coming over. I'd like to introduce you. Is that okay?"

"Sure. I know them, but I don't talk to them a lot."

"Used to be Sweet Water seemed a lot smaller than it is now, which I suppose is a good thing, but I guess it takes a little longer to get to know everyone. Unless you've grown up here, like I have."

"Although you don't live that close, right?"

He nodded in agreement, but he didn't have a chance to say anything more when the group got to them, and one of the guys put his hand on his shoulder.

"I guess you won the bet we had," the man said.

"Gordon," Beau said with a warning note in his voice, but it was too late. Claudia's heart had stopped. He sat with her because of a bet? Had he been so friendly to her because of it too? Is that why he had gone to the ensemble the night before? What was it about?

"What, bro? She digs you. It's okay." Gordon grinned at Claudia. "I know you like him, but when you first came, you didn't seem to, and he and I made a bet that you wouldn't talk to him for at least five years. That was after he told you something about your hair and an electrical socket."

She remembered that, in Technicolor detail. It wasn't exactly a comment that a woman forgot easily. But she pushed it aside because she had said some things to him that weren't exactly kind either. She didn't want him to hold that against her, but a bet was a completely different story.

"That's not why I'm talking to you now," Beau said hurriedly, as though he was trying to head off what he was afraid was going to be a terrible confrontation. Of course.

"Really? That's odd, since, even as recently as Friday morning, when I was chasing the pigs around, you were rather rude. But I guess that shows I really am as gullible as everybody says. I believed you when you acted like you wanted us to put the past behind us and start new. That was kind of dumb of me, wasn't it?" She sounded rather fatalistic and dramatic, but she couldn't help it. In the last twenty-four hours, she had decided that she liked him. And even better than that, she thought he liked her.

She wanted to leave immediately. But she didn't want to run out with her tail between her legs and let him know exactly how much this hurt her.

Maybe she felt like a fool, more than she hurt, although the feelings were pretty much equal.

"Claudia. I promise. It's not what it sounds like."

"Really? So you guys didn't have a bet?"

"It was five years ago. I mean, you weren't even living here full-time. Although we all knew your family was planning on moving in."

"Really?"

It didn't really matter how long ago it was. He spent the last five years being unkind, and then he'd figured out where she was vulnerable and pounced.

"Yeah." He paused, and then he straightened up a little, like he was afraid she was going to lash out at him. "Have I ever lied? Is that my reputation in town?"

She closed her mouth and looked away. He really did have a good reputation. One of character and of integrity. Plus, he helped his dad on the ranch and got along with him. That was a testament to both father and son. A lot of times, those types of relationships didn't work out, where the son wanted something different, or the father pushed too hard. But the fact that they could both get along said a lot about the character of each.

"He's right. It was a long time ago, and I was just joking about it. I'm sorry." Gordon looked truly upset, and Claudia almost felt bad for him.

Beau jerked his head, and the group walked away, leaving him standing there with Claudia as churchgoers mingled around them moving slowly toward the door.

"He's right. There was a bet. But it was...not on my mind today. I promise." He blew out a breath. "It seems like every time I try to get a little closer to you, some kind of weird roadblock comes up that just blows up into some kind of misunderstanding. Can we... Can we decide we're not going to let that happen?"

He sounded...sincere. But she knew a lot of good actors. People who could say one thing while meaning another the entire time. People who would say whatever they needed to in order to get their way.

She was familiar with that and suspected that that might be happening, but at the same time, he was right. If he was sincere, she was really wrong to take something and run with it, without working things out.

Except, she wouldn't even have considered them friends before yesterday. Was it really even necessary for her to work things out with someone she wasn't friends with?

But if she were honest, she wanted to be.

"You're right. I'm sorry. I... I guess that's pretty hurtful when you think someone is only being nice to you to win a bet. How much was it for?"

"Honestly, I don't even remember. He mentioned it this morning, and he probably saw that it irritated me, and so he came over here, deciding that he was going to pick on me a little more. I know he didn't do it to upset you. Gordon's not like that."

She liked the way he defended his friend and took the blame for himself. It...showed humility and an honesty that was lacking in a lot of people.

She nodded. "I see. So... I guess that's just a little hurtful. You know?"

"I know. It was stupid. I'd love to say that I've outgrown all those kinds of things, but unfortunately, I do stupid things pretty much every day. Even though I try hard to learn from them and make sure that I don't continue to be as dumb tomorrow as I am today."

"No. You don't need to call yourself dumb. I do stupid stuff too. I think we all do. It's a human thing."

"Yeah. I... I sent you flowers on Friday. I was afraid to sign my name."

"Afraid?" she said, thinking of the beautiful bouquet that was sitting on her dresser. They were from Beau. That explained the B.

"Yeah. We're not exactly great friends, but when I heard about your dog, it made me sad. I had a dog I loved growing up, and I was pretty devastated when she passed. Actually, I said at the time I was never getting another dog. I just didn't want one."

"I understand. We used Ginger on the ranch all the time, until she got too old. We have other dogs, but she went with me everywhere. I guess I do want another dog, even though I'm afraid that it won't be fair to whatever I get, because I'll always be comparing her to Ginger."

"That happens, doesn't it?"

"What? Comparisons?"

"Yeah. I think that's the human thing too. We compare everything —this year with last year, the rain we got this year with the rain we got last year, the calves we have this year with the calves we had last year, the tractor I'm driving now versus the tractor my dad drove when he was my age, you know, all those things."

"The girlfriend you have now versus the girlfriend you had ten years ago."

"Yeah, that would be a little bit tough, since I really haven't had many girlfriends. I guess I was focused more on farming than I was on family. But you're right. You have a tendency to compare."

"Which is probably a good argument for not having one until you're ready to settle down. After all, if you know you're not in the market for a family, what's the point?"

"I agree with that." He seemed to pause, and she really didn't know what to say. She didn't want to continue talking about that with him. She believed him when he said that he hadn't meant for her to be hurt over the bet, but it was still a little bit fresh in her mind, and the idea that she might not be able to trust him was there too. While she agreed that they should talk about things and generally assumed the best about someone, she also thought that there were probably people that it was best if she just said hi and bye to and didn't try to develop a deeper relationship with.

To her, Beau was one of those people. They'd just never been able to get along, and although she felt...something for him, something she really couldn't put a name to, something she wasn't sure she wanted to put a name to actually, because it felt an awful lot like attraction, or like curiosity, the kind of interest that drew her to someone, and she really resisted that. She didn't want to be more than casual acquaintances with him. It didn't feel safe.

Of course, maybe she shouldn't spend her life trying to be safe.

She looked over and saw both his parents, Ford and Morgan Hansen, in the back of the church by the door, looking around, perhaps to see if their son was near.

Morgan was absolutely beautiful, even though she must have been in her forties or fifties. And Ford had been handsome at one time. His face had been marred by a farm accident, but their genetics had certainly produced a handsome son.

Yeah, she could admit that Beau was handsome.

Chapter Eleven

"So, what are you doing this afternoon?" Beau said, after a few moments of silence as they followed the crowd toward the back of the church.

Claudia spoke as they inched forward. "Typically on Sunday, my family tries to eat together. There are so many of us, and the farmhouse wasn't big enough for us all to live together, but we try to get together on Sundays." She hesitated before saying more. He wasn't her friend, and she didn't really want to tell him everything that was going on in her life, but her mouth seemed to open of its own accord, and she continued to talk. "We get our first guests for our dude ranch tomorrow. So we'll be talking about that too."

"Wow. That started already?"

"Yeah. We're just trying to get as much income going on the ranch as we can."

"I knew your brothers were doing cattle, and they had some crops as well. And I talked to Tobias. He said that you guys were getting things fixed up for guests, but he neglected to mention they were coming so soon."

"That's Tobias. He neglects to mention a lot." Claudia laughed, because Tobias was notoriously quiet and had become even more so after the incident in his life that had changed him.

She pressed her lips together and tried not to think about it. Tobias had grown from that, and she truly felt like he was becoming a better person. But no one should have to go through something like that.

"All right. Well, my mom is waving at me, so I probably better walk over. I'm still on the ranch, so it's not like she doesn't see me every day, but since I moved out of the house ten years ago, every time she sees me out somewhere, she acts like we haven't seen each other for years."

"Because she loves you. I'd tell you to appreciate your parents, but I think you probably do."

He stopped, and a thoughtful expression crossed his face. "I guess that's the kind of advice someone like you could tell me, and it's good." He nodded. "Sorry about your parents."

"It's been long enough ago that it's not that big of a deal. I mean, I don't think I'll ever get over it, but just... It's nice to see that your mom cares about you."

She didn't really want to say anything else. It had been ten years, but she still missed her parents. At this point, she thought she probably always would. There were so many things that she would think that she wanted to tell her mom, she wanted to share with them, or she wanted to know what they thought or...just wanted to talk to them.

At least, when their parents died, her family had stayed together. Sometimes it seemed like the parents were the only things holding everything together, and once they were gone, the kids just kinda split up into their own factions.

She supposed Ezra was the main person they needed to thank for that, although Phoebe and Priscilla had always worked to keep the family together as well.

She tried as hard as she could to help, especially since she knew what a sacrifice it was for Priscilla to be in North Dakota.

"Yeah. I need to appreciate that," he finally murmured, and then he lifted his hand as though he was going to touch her, but then it dropped to his side without him moving it toward her at all. "Thanks for sitting with me. I...haven't enjoyed a church service like that in a long time."

"Thanks for letting me. I guess I could have sat on the floor in the back."

He grinned. "It wasn't that full. But they just built this church a little over a decade ago, and they're already outgrowing it. They might need to think about getting another building."

"Or having two services."

Different churches had done that. But it was a little bit sad because then a person didn't get to see their whole church family.

He nodded and then hesitated as though he were loath to leave her or had something else he wanted to say.

She could hardly believe the first, and the second didn't seem likely as well since he turned and walked away without saying anything more.

She was tempted to watch him go as he moved through the pew and over toward his parents. But she averted her eyes and continued to move slowly toward the door. She didn't want to want to watch him. She wanted to be as unaffected by him as he seemed to be by her.

Sure, he seemed to be going out of his way to make sure that they weren't antagonistic toward each other, which she supposed on some level she appreciated, but she didn't want to be all chummy with him. Since she'd moved into Sweet Water, they'd been nothing but antagonistic, even enemies. She couldn't just flip a switch and all of a sudden want to be best friends with someone whom she thought hated her up until that point.

Forgive, as I have forgiven you.

She didn't even really think she had anything to forgive. She just had feelings of reluctance to overcome. Maybe she needed to work a little harder on that.

She shook the pastor's hand and didn't see Beau again after she left, but she did meet back up with her sisters Ada and Joanna. Her youngest sister, Lois, was still in college and had been offered an internship position over the summer. She hadn't decided whether she was coming back to the ranch yet or not.

Joanna was with Stonewall, of course. Since the two had been inseparable since birth. Stonewall had even moved from Wyoming to North Dakota when they did, and they hired him on the ranch. They were a package deal, and Joanna pretty much didn't do anything without Stonewall with her.

More than once, Claudia had wondered what in the world would happen when one of them got married. If it were her, she certainly wouldn't want to be married to a man who was best friends with another woman. And she assumed that no man would want to be married to a woman who was best friends with another man, but then again, she supposed in the modern day that was much more likely to happen. Even though it felt not quite right to her. As a wife, she would not want her husband to know another woman better than he did her. Or to like someone or respect them more. Which is what could potentially happen when one had a best friend of the opposite gender.

Regardless, there was no romance between the two of them, they were just...like brother and sister.

Since the farmhouse hadn't been big enough to house them all, and since Joanna was young enough to still want to push for a little bit of independence and spread her wings some, she and Stonewall had rented opposite sides of an old farmhouse that had been turned into a duplex not far from the Sweet View Ranch. There wasn't a lot of acreage with it, and they both worked on the ranch, they just had a little bit of elbow room.

"I know you said you were cooking all the food, but I just want to see if you needed us to stop at the grocery store for anything on our way out to the ranch?" Joanna said as Claudia walked toward them in the parking lot.

"No. It should be good. I have a crockpot of sloppy joes and French fries ready that I'll stick in the oven when I get there." It was warm enough that they were all going to be eating out in the bunkhouse. In the winter, they didn't get together as often, because there wasn't enough room in the farmhouse and it was too cold to be outside.

The bunkhouse wasn't heated, although they were working on fixing that, since it would give them a little bit more time to operate their dude ranch.

"All right. We're going to stop at our house and change our clothes, and then we'll be out," Joanna said.

Ada slipped her hand through Claudia's arm, and they walked side by side.

"Those two. I don't know when they're going to see that they're absolutely perfect for each other."

"You think?" Claudia said, scrunching up her brows and watching as Joanna and Stonewall bantered with each other as they walked away. Her laughter rang out as he shoved his hands in his pockets and lifted his shoulder. She couldn't see his face, but she imagined it would have a grin on it.

"Yeah. For sure. He definitely is totally infatuated with her. But I don't think she notices, and she really takes advantage of him sometimes."

"Yeah. I've noticed that. She does seem to just assume that he's always going to be there. I mean, when we decided we were moving to North Dakota, she just assumed he was going. Now of course he did, but...sometimes I think she just doesn't appreciate what a blessing it is to have such a good, loyal friend."

"Yeah. I don't think he's going to wait around forever though. At some point, he's going to decide that he needs to find someone. They're still young though. Maybe they'll figure things out."

Claudia nodded and didn't say anything. Ada was five years older than she was, but since their parents died, the age difference hadn't seemed to matter as much. Especially since Claudia had graduated from high school. It seemed like when a person was an adult, age differences didn't matter as much as character and integrity did.

"I have to ice the Texas sheet cake I made, and then I'll be over to help you grill the eggplant."

"Thanks. I have everything mixed up ahead of time that I can, but I didn't cut the eggplants because they get brown."

"I know. They're better fresh anyway."

Eggplant was a sort of splurge for their family. Everyone loved it, but it wasn't something that was cheap in North Dakota. It was way too cold to grow them, so while it wasn't quite exotic, it was definitely a treat.

They cooked it a little differently than most people might have, since they always grilled it. Then they had different toppings that they had with it.

As far as Claudia was concerned, if eggplant was the only thing they had for lunch, it would be enough. But her brothers usually wanted some kind of meat, and hence the sloppy joes. French fries were always a hit too. And they would go well with the sauces they were making for the eggplant.

She and Ada drove home, chatting the whole time. There were plenty of things to talk about since their first dude ranch guests would arrive the next day.

Lucas pulled in behind them with Phoebe and Priscilla in his pickup, and Claudia had barely gotten out of her car when Lucas called over, "When's the wedding?"

She knew that was going to be something that people were going to tease her about if she sat with Beau during church.

She ignored her brother, since she found that was usually the best policy, and continued toward the house.

Lucas was two years older than she was, and she'd been teased by him mercilessly growing up. Of course, she had done her own teasing in return, and it was one of the reasons why she felt that having siblings was so good for a person. It taught them to give and to take, and gave them some insight into how human relationships work.

When a person didn't have siblings, when their siblings were not very close in age, she supposed they could still develop personal skills, it just wasn't as natural.

Regardless, Lucas and she had grown into really great friends, and she was probably closer to him than she was to any of her other siblings. They had similar personalities. They were both extroverts who enjoyed time by themselves but really loved the big, crowded family.

Poor Tobias, being an introvert in a family of twelve siblings. It must have been hard.

She wasn't even sure he would come today, except since they were expecting guests the next day, he would probably show up, hang around the back, throw a few thoughts out that no one else had considered, ones that would stop everyone in their tracks, and then slip away.

Of course, Phoebe was an introvert as well, but Tobias definitely had the title of the one who disliked the big, noisy family gatherings.

She threw the French fries in the oven and grabbed the eggplant out of the fridge.

The crockpots were already over in the bunkhouse, and the grill was over there as well. She would cut the eggplant up, pull the moisture from them by salting them for a few minutes, take them over and stick them on the grill, and come back and get the French fries out of the oven. She'd done enough cooking for a whole crowd of people that it was kind of second nature to just do things so they worked.

"What's the matter, sis? Cat got your tongue?" Lucas said when he came in the door, laughing as he walked over and put his arm around her. "Do I need to talk to Beau about being his best man? After all, I'm your favorite brother."

"You're one of my six favorite brothers," she said, reaching up and patting him on the head. He had always been taller than she was, since he was two years older, but it was a bit more of a stretch now than it used to be.

"It's okay, Claude, just tell him you're getting married next Saturday so he can show up to the church and be there by himself for a while," Rufus said, coming in behind Lucas with a little less fanfare.

Rufus was two years younger than she was, and while she wouldn't have minded having a sister beside her in birth order, being sandwiched between the two boys hadn't been terrible.

"That's a good idea. Maybe just pretend to have a big wedding, although I suppose I could invite the whole town and let them know Lucas is getting married."

"I am?" Lucas said, dipping a finger in one of the covered containers she had in the refrigerator.

"Would you stop? We are going to eat very soon, I promise. You're not going to waste away to nothing until we get there."

"I'm just tasting it. Making sure that you're not trying to poison us with something. That's pretty much my job, isn't it? I'm the expendable one."

"You're not expendable, Lucas. But you just stuck dirty fingers into my food."

"My fingers aren't dirty. I washed them two days ago. With soap."

She sighed, acting put out, but she really didn't mind. With a family as big as theirs, working on a ranch and growing up there, no one could get too excited about germs. They certainly had shared each other's germs often enough that it probably didn't matter. It was just the idea.

"When we have guests, you're definitely not going to be able to do that." She gave him her best serious sister look, although as the younger sister, it was always hard to get respect.

"Yes, ma'am," he said, winking at her.

Mina bounced into the kitchen. "I have my clothes changed. Can I help?"

"Of course you can. I have some things you can carry over to the bunkhouse, and do not allow Lucas to convince you to let him stick his fingers in any of them." She gave Lucas the hairy eyeball, which he just grinned at and came over, putting an arm around her so that she was in a headlock while he kissed the side of her temple.

"You love me. You know it."

"I do, but you're incorrigible."

"I'm pretty sure that's a compliment." He hesitated. "So, I don't suppose you have any books you'd like me to borrow from the library for you, do you?"

"What?"

"You know, books. Those hard, rectangular things that you read."

"When did you figure out what those things were?"

"I've known what they were for a long time now. At least a year or two."

"You're hilarious. Library? When did you get interested in the library?" Of all of their siblings, Lucas was the one who wanted to be up interacting and talking to people. He could never be bothered to sit still long enough to actually read a book.

"Well, since I saw the cute librarian."

"Really? We are embarking on a new venture, having our first guests tomorrow, and all of a sudden, you're gonna be chasing some poor woman around the library? Be kind to the librarian and just leave her alone."

"But you didn't see her. I'm telling you, she's cute. I mean, I'm not saying anything, but...I think she likes me."

Claudia laughed outright at that. "What makes you think that? Did she find you a book you could borrow?"

"No. She looked at me."

"She looked at you... And now you think she likes you?"

"Sure. The last fifteen times I've been there, she hasn't looked up at all, but today... She looked at me. I definitely need to visit the library again. Soon. So, what would you like me to check out for you?"

"This is going to be a novel idea, Lucas, so listen closely," Claudia said as she sliced the last eggplant into big, thick pieces. "How about you get a book out for yourself?"

Chapter Twelve

"Mina?" Lucas said as Mina came back in the door. "Wouldn't you like a book from the library? In fact, you and I could take a trip to the library. Wouldn't that be fun?"

Lucas said it in such a way that Claudia had to laugh, because Lucas's idea of fun was definitely not taking a trip to the library. His infatuation with the library would blow over like a summer thunderstorm. Although, he had said the last ten or fifteen times that he walked by her...

This infatuation had lasted longer than any of his other ones. Still, because it was Lucas, she doubted it would last long. He was going to need someone who could talk more than he could. He definitely wouldn't allow a quiet, shy, retiring librarian to get a word in edgewise.

He and Mina chatted about libraries, and books, until Lucas successfully changed the subject to dirt bike racing, which was much more his speed, as Claudia covered the eggplant and pushed her way out the door.

She loved her family and enjoyed being around them, but she also sometimes wondered what it would be like to be married and have a home of her own, with just her and her husband. It would be quiet, cozy, fun... Maybe they'd live on the ranch, maybe they wouldn't, but they'd definitely want a house of their own.

She nodded at Ezra as he came out of the other house, Alice, the baby, in his arm, his other hand around his wife, who held the hand of her young son.

They seemed like they settled down and were quite cozy in the small house that was just a few steps away from the big farmhouse.

Whoever had built that hadn't wanted to move very far away from their family.

Claudia had laughed sometimes at how close the house was. What was the point in even moving out?

She chatted with Alaska and Ezra as they walked toward the bunkhouse.

"Is Bernice coming?" she asked, knowing that Alaska talked to Bernice, the lady who had been their nanny growing up, far more than she did, since Bernice often watched their children for them so Alaska could help Ezra with the bookwork for the ranch.

"I don't think so. She said something about getting together with the ladies at the Olympic training center. I think they have some things up their sleeve, and Bernice wanted to be a part of the whole event."

"I don't know if we should let her hang around those ladies. They seem like they might get themselves into a bit of trouble."

"I think at that age, it's okay to have a little fun. Especially in the name of benevolence. Because they do help people, they just...don't do it in quite the traditional way." Ezra grinned, and Claudia was so happy to see his smile. He had been very serious, shouldering the burdens of the family since her parents had died, and it seemed like his smiles had been fewer and far between until he met Alaska.

Claudia would never have picked Alaska out as being Ezra's perfect match, but she certainly seemed to bring out the lighter side of him.

They chatted as they walked into the bunkhouse, Claudia seeing that Mina and Lucas had arranged the things they carried over. Lucas enjoyed teasing her, and sometimes his outgoing and goofy personality made him seem a little younger than what he was, but he was just as responsible as any of her other brothers.

There was definitely a soft spot in her heart for him.

Her family chatted as she ran back over to grab the French fries, passing Ada carrying her Texas sheet cake across. She had just made one, and it would probably be gone by the time lunch was over. If they continue to get married and have children, it was going to take two sheet cakes for each dinner, but Claudia knew it was probably just wishful thinking on her part that the entire family would stay together.

In fact, she passed Priscilla on her way, and her heart squeezed.

Priscilla hadn't made it to church, and it was obvious that she'd been crying. Her eyes were red rimmed, her nose puffy, but she just waved away Claudia's concerned look and continued to walk.

She probably wouldn't want to talk about it, but Claudia guessed that it had to do with her children. Priscilla's divorce had not been amicable, although Priscilla had tried as hard as she could to get along with her ex. He'd lied to her, constantly, and had agreed when Priscilla moved from Wyoming that they would continue to share the children equally. For a while the kids had even been on the farm, attending school in their district.

But her ex had been difficult and deceitful and had gone behind Priscilla's back to gain full custody of the kids.

She knew Priscilla was torn, wanting to stay with her family and continue to build what their parents had started, but desperately missing her children, and she ended up spending a lot of her time on the road, driving back to Wyoming. Which she had known she was going to have to do, but her ex hadn't come to what she thought had been their agreement.

Claudia breathed out, wishing there was something she could do, but sometimes life just hurt.

Of course, Priscilla, out of all of her siblings, was the one she prayed for the most. At least, she was one who seemed like she needed the most prayer currently.

But if the death of her parents had taught her anything, she thought as she pulled the French fries out of the oven and carefully scraped them into a large bowl and covered them with a towel, it had taught her that life could turn in an instant. And she should never take anything for granted. Not today, not the idea that there would be a tomorrow, and not the memories that they made, any times they were able to get together and share each other's company.

The pain went through her at the thought of her parents being able to be here, to see how they turned out.

Of course there had been hard times. Of course they'd made mistakes.

She pushed the door open with her elbow and stepped in. Her eyes fell again on Priscilla, who chatted with Caleb and Phoebe along the edge.

They all gathered around the tables, and Ezra said a prayer.

After they had passed most of the food and started eating, they chatted about the guests that were coming and the different things that they needed to do in order to get ready.

Lucas was the most outgoing, and he was the one who would be leading the trail rides and entertaining the guests for the most part. He was also the least organized, and so it didn't totally shock Claudia when he called out to her from the other end of the table.

"Hey, Claude? I assumed it would be okay for you to lead some singing every evening around the campfire. I mean, you've learned, what, six chords on the guitar or something?"

She'd been working on the guitar, even though Ezra could play really well. Since he had Alaska, and the children, they all assumed that he wouldn't be available most evenings to entertain guests, unless his family could be with him.

"I can. Any night except for Saturday nights. I have ensemble practice then." She looked around at her siblings. Her mom had made sure that every one of them could play some kind of instrument. "Which, by the way, all of you are invited to."

She knew they probably wouldn't come. Not in the summer. If she had it over the winter, they would probably make sure they made it, but all of them were busy, and she kind of regretted the fact that she thought that it had been a good idea to go ahead and start one. Even though she did think it would be something for the guests to do in town. It had been a good idea, just not something she had time for and not something that people apparently were interested in helping her with.

Except for Beau.

Whether or not his cousins would come was anyone's guess.

Actually, she guessed not. It seemed to her that they were just talking about the bet that they'd had and maybe making fun of him a little bit. She almost would bet money on the fact that they had zero intention of coming to her orchestra.

She'd find out on Saturday.

Putting Beau out of her mind, although making a mental note that she needed to try to order some music, she looked back over at Lucas.

"But, Claude, Saturday is the most important night! We actually have five extra guests who were just coming for Friday and Saturday nights."

"You are doing a sermon on Saturday, right?" Lucas looked at Tobias, who had managed to show up, although he hadn't said anything so far.

"Yeah," he said, kind of slow, like he didn't really want to, but he was planning on it. Of all of them, Tobias had a more solid grip on doctrine and a life that had proven that he really lived what he believed.

People couldn't go through what he had, with the kind of character that he had shown, without gaining a reputation, especially among the people who were closest to him, for truly being exactly what he said he was.

He looked up at her. "You can come back after orchestra practice. You were home by seven o'clock the last time. That's plenty of time to make it out to the campfire and do some songs from eight to nine."

If it had been Lucas telling her that, she would have argued. But Tobias had a calm, commanding way about him. Even though he was technically the fifth child.

He should have been the peacemaker, which he was, but somehow he also had that kind of personality where he didn't even have to talk loud, but everybody listened. He always seemed wiser than his years.

Although no one was perfect, and he had definitely made a big mistake.

Still, Claudia cherished the afternoon together. She figured that things would get busy over the summer, with them trying to go in all kinds of different directions, although one direction that had been near and dear to her heart were horses. But the family had decided that they had enough going on, and when she had suggested it, they had shut down that idea.

It took a lot of time in order to make money from any equine endeavor, because typically it was a well-trained horse that would bring in the big money, and none of them were going to have time to train horses.

Claudia had some different ideas, but...sometimes a person had to give up what they wanted for the good of the group, and this felt like something that she had to let go of. For now. Sure, they were her favorite animal, and she'd loved them since she was little, and the whole family could ride, but she knew her brothers were right. They had a tendency to cost more money than they made.

"I was thinking we should try to put on a rodeo. Maybe this fall, although if we can't have it by then, in the spring or next summer for sure." Caleb spoke, and everyone turned to look at him.

Claudia hadn't considered a rodeo, but it seemed like a really great idea.

"I'm in!" she said.

She had barely gotten her words out when her siblings echoed them. Everyone seemed pretty enthused about the idea, and after some discussion, they had decided that they would try to do it that fall. Maybe September, before it got too cold.

Claudia felt that for the most part, her life was really looking up. Sure, the orchestra had been a disaster, and she wasn't sure whether she could trust Beau or not, and she was going to be busier that summer than she ever had been in her life before, with the financial stability of the ranch depending on not just her, but all of them.

Still, she should be over-the-moon happy, so she wasn't quite sure why that nagging sense of missing something wouldn't go away.

Chapter Thirteen

"Let's get her cooled down, then I'd like to make sure she gets in the stall tonight. I want to keep an eye on that hoof. I don't like the way that crack's looking." Beau slapped his hand against his jeans and nodded at Silver's right front hoof.

Herbert nodded. He was an older ranch hand, someone who had been with his dad for decades, and Beau had grown up with him.

"You got it, boss." He didn't even say "boss" with a sarcastic lift of his brow. He really did give Beau the respect that his position deserved. Of course, he was the owner's son, but he worked just as long and as hard as everyone else, and had since he was young.

He walked away from Herbert after handing Silver's lead over to him. He wanted to go look at the geldings that he had been working with and think about the things he needed to focus on this week.

His thoughts had been a little muddled since he ran into Claudia. And her piglets. Then went to ensemble practice and sat with her in church.

He couldn't seem to stop thinking about her, and every time his brain had a little bit of space, his thoughts were filled with excuses for visiting her family ranch.

He and Tobias were pretty good friends, and they talked every few days at the very least.

Tobias actually didn't talk a whole lot, but he had the kind of wisdom that Beau appreciated and felt drawn toward. He felt like he was good friends with Lucas as well, although Lucas and his friendship was more of a casual, fun type of friendship rather than a serious work relationship, the way he felt about Tobias.

Regardless, whether it was for fun or for work, he couldn't figure out how he could get to the Clybourns without it being obvious.

All of them were going to be suspicious since he sat beside Claudia in church. He still couldn't believe she had voluntarily gone to his pew with him. But she had been a little cool afterward, and he couldn't blame her. The idea that there might have been some kind of bet, that he was just setting her up to make fun of her was pretty nasty, although from the way the relationship had started, he couldn't blame her for believing it. He wanted to strangle Gordon for even suggesting it, but Gordon hadn't meant anything by it.

And honestly, if he and Claudia had a better relationship, she would have laughed it off. He was sure about it. She didn't seem like the kind of person who got offended over everything.

It had been two days, and he would have thought that he could get his head on straight by now, but he hadn't. Which he probably should be worried about. He didn't typically get distracted like this, and it wasn't the best way to work. A man should be focused on what he was supposed to be doing, rather than allowing himself to daydream about what might be with a woman who didn't even really consider him a friend.

He leaned on the railing, looking at his blue roan, which was his favorite of the geldings he was working with. Blue Moon was his registered name, but Beau called him Mooney. Not exactly a manly name, but sometimes nicknames were given and a person didn't have much say in them. Or his horse.

Mooney was smart and a quick learner, and eager to do what he'd been bred to do. Beau was thinking about that and was startled when his phone began to ring.

He pulled it out of his pocket, saw that it was one of his older sisters, Norma, and he smiled before answering.

"Hello?" he said, always happy to hear from one of his sisters.

"So when is the wedding, little bro?" she said, the humor in her voice easy to hear.

"Wow. You're really behind the times. That was like forty-eight hours ago."

"You got married two days ago?"

"No, I apparently announced to the town that I was going to get married two days ago, when I sat with a girl who is not even technically one of my friends in church."

"You should definitely not get married to someone you're not friends with. The best marriages have a strong friendship as a solid foundation."

"So did you just call to lecture me on what makes a good marriage? Or did you actually have something you wanted to talk to me about?"

"I heard from Gordon that you're doing an ensemble, and I just couldn't believe it."

"I'm participating in an ensemble. The person that I sat with in church is actually doing it."

"Oh." She drew the word out. "That explains everything."

"Everything? What are you talking about?"

"Well, I thought it was weird that you were sitting with this girl in church, someone I've never heard of."

"She moved in after you got married and moved away."

His sister didn't live that far away, about an hour's drive to the north, where her husband worked in oil. He thought eventually they would come back to the farm, but for now, her husband's job kept them away.

"I see. Well, I thought it weird you were doing some kind of orchestra, even though I know you play the French horn and you were quite good at it. You had one year you loved it, and then you had other interests, so...it seemed a little suspicious when you all of a sudden got interested in the French horn again."

"I like music. Always have." He tried to defend himself, but he knew she was right. The only reason he was interested in the orchestra was because Claudia was doing it. Otherwise, he would do the same thing everyone else in town had done and think that maybe he would support them by going but not actually by participating in it.

"Right, Beaumont," she said, using his full name, like he supposed an older sister had a right to do.

"You just called to give me a hard time, is that right?" he asked, and she laughed.

"Yeah. Don't you remember how much you teased me when Ranger was courting me? My goodness, you hid around every corner, spying on us, just so you could take a picture of us kissing so you could show it to Mom and Dad. Like I was getting in trouble for kissing my fiancé."

"I was a turkey, wasn't I?"

"You sure were. And I owe you. Plus..." Her voice changed. "I care. Truly. And I like talking to you."

"I like talking to you too. And I know you care. But it's nice to hear from you, even if the only time you call is when you're making fun of me."

"Well, what can I help you with today? That way, the call isn't totally about making fun of you, and I can do something helpful."

"If you really want to help me, you can tell me what kind of excuse I can make up so that I can go over to the Clybourns, and it won't seem like I'm just doing it because I want to see Claudia."

"But in reality, you're just doing it because you want to see Claudia." She sounded serious. "Just making sure."

"Yeah. That's terrible, isn't it?"

"Why don't you just ask her out the way a normal person would?"

"I don't think her family is normal."

"She's the one with twelve kids in the family?"

"Yeah."

"Yeah. You're right. She's not normal."

"See?"

"Yeah. Well, you probably want to do something with the whole family then. Those big families, they all want to stick together and hang out, like their own little town or something."

"That's kinda cool. I wish our parents had had more children."

"I know Mom wanted to. I don't think she could."

Beau was quiet. He hadn't really talked about that with his parents. But he supposed that would make sense. They had been such great parents, sometimes he wondered why they hadn't raised more children. But maybe they wanted to and they just hadn't been able. He could talk to his dad about it, but he probably wouldn't say anything to his mom. From the tone of Norma's voice, it was a sore subject for her.

"That's too bad." He'd always wanted a brother. Of course, he and his dad had a strong relationship, it felt unbreakable to him. And maybe he wouldn't have been quite as close to his dad if there had been more kids in their family. Although, he had a feeling his dad would have made sure that he had a good relationship with all of his kids. His dad was just that way.

"Anyway, you know something I think would make Mom happier than almost anything would be to have a whole pile of grandkids. If Claudia comes from a family of twelve, maybe she'd want to have a whole bunch. You should ask her."

"Yeah. I might not be the greatest with relationships, but I can say for sure that talking about the number of children you want to have is not a good way to start things out."

"Why not? You're not talking about superficial things that don't really matter, you're getting right to the heart of things, so you know whether you're compatible or not."

"Who said it was wise for me to get advice from you?"

"Fine. Maybe I don't want to see my baby brother married just yet."

"Don't you think I'm mature enough?" he said as Mooney moseyed over and stood by the railing, asking to have his ear scratched.

"Oh, you're more than mature enough. It just makes me feel old. But I do want to see you happy, and Claudia sounds like a really nice girl. You want me to drive down with the kids, and I can get lost on their ranch, and I can call you to come find me, and you could just happen to run into her?"

"Somehow your ideas just keep getting worse and worse. How did you and Ranger ever get together?"

"He chased me till I caught him, and that's the truth."

Beau laughed, thinking that it probably was pretty close to the truth. Ranger had been crazy about Norma, and Norma had been caught between following a modeling career, the way her mom had, or giving it all up and getting married. Ranger had made a pretty persuasive case, and it was obvious that the two of them were deeply in love.

"Do you regret giving up the opportunity to model?" he asked, knowing that for a while, Norma had put all of her spare time into traveling and doing whatever it took to build her career.

"No. It wasn't for me. That is just not the culture that I want to be involved in. I'm glad Ranger came along and helped me open my eyes. I was pretty fixated on it, and I wasn't listening to what the Lord wanted me to do."

He didn't say anything for a while, figuring that maybe he was a little bit of the same. He didn't want to get so fixated on the things that he wanted out of his life that he didn't do what God wanted him to.

Maybe that was why he was so drawn to Claudia. She didn't seem like the kind of girl he might be interested in, especially since she wasn't interested in him to begin with. Typically he didn't go chasing girls around who acted like they'd rather he kept a ten-mile radius between them.

He supposed it could be the challenge too, although that was less than likely in his opinion.

"You know, though. They're starting that dude ranch, you could offer to help them somehow. Do you know what they're doing? I mean, you and Dad have some of the best horses in the state. Do they need horses?"

"Our horses aren't exactly the kind of horses that they'd be using. But... I don't know. Maybe I could figure something out."

He tried to think of something but couldn't come up with anything else.

"Why don't you call and see if they'll give you a job. Just volunteer to help. You know, be neighborly."

He laughed, but he supposed Norma was right. If he wanted to go over, he shouldn't make up an excuse, he should find something he could help with.

"All right. I guess I might as well. I don't really have anything to lose. The worst they could do is say no, but who turns down free help?"

"Exactly. And who knows. You just might get paired up with Claudia. Maybe one of them is a matchmaker."

He laughed, and he and Norma talked for a couple more minutes before he hung up.

He decided he'd call Tobias. Like he just said, he didn't have anything to lose. So what if they figured out that he was interested in Claudia? That wasn't a crime, and other than possibly being a little bit embarrassing that she didn't return his interest, there was no risk involved. If she didn't like him or wasn't interested in him the way he was interested in her, it wasn't going to be the end of the world.

Although, he had a feeling that he was going to be more disappointed than what he let on.

Chapter Fourteen

Claudia put her guitar in the back of the wagon hooked to a tractor and then went over to Boxer, one of their ranch horses, that she'd saddled earlier. Other than cooking and cleaning and doing laundry, she hadn't helped with the guests much at all, but it was Friday night, and Caleb had specifically asked her if she'd be there to play the guitar around the campfire.

The guests had left earlier, right after lunch, and Claudia had stayed behind, making the things that they would have around the campfire for supper and packing them up. The wagon was loaded. Rather than drive in with the pickup, they decided it would be a little more rustic and enjoyable for the guests if they took a tractor. Plus, she was going to ride her horse and would be out later.

From what she could see, things had been going well that week, and the guests seemed to be having a good time.

She'd seen a couple posts on social media, and that had been encouraging as well, since word of mouth and social proof were both good advertisements for their ranch.

She couldn't wait until tomorrow, though, because Alaska and Mina were going to cook breakfast, and she had the day off. Everyone had at least one day off each week; they decided that from the start.

Some of them would have to work on Sundays, so they would stagger their days throughout the week. Claudia's day had just happened to land on Saturday, which worked really well, since she would have to take time off to do orchestra in the afternoon anyway.

Her music had arrived, and she was excited about it, thinking that she had overreacted, and that things were actually going to work out.

She was just thinking that as she checked Boxer's girth, when a pickup drove into the parking area, and she furrowed her brows.

They weren't supposed to be getting any new guests, not until tomorrow. They had a few extra people coming for just one night. But...

The pickup looked like Beau's.

He pulled into the barn, and she watched Tobias walk out, and she turned back to her horse.

She wasn't close enough that she could shout a greeting to him, even if she wanted to.

Which, she told herself, she didn't. She had things she needed to do, she needed to get to the campfire and lead the singing. That was the first thing on her mind.

Then, having a little bit of downtime tomorrow before she had to go to lead the ensemble was the second.

She had grocery shopping she needed to do, which technically wasn't something that she should have to do in her downtime, but she just hadn't had time throughout the week to do it, and they had more guests coming tomorrow and the next week.

She mounted Boxer and started off toward where the campfire was going to be that evening. It was a couple of miles northeast, and thankfully, that was the exact opposite direction of where Beau spoke with Tobias.

It was about ten minutes later when she heard horse hooves behind her and shifted in her saddle. Had Beau brought news? Why wouldn't Tobias have just called her?

She couldn't seem to get Beau out of her brain and welcomed whatever distraction it was going to be.

Until she turned and saw Beau was in the saddle.

He rode Hank, one of her favorite horses. He was a little hard to handle at times, even though she considered herself an experienced horsewoman, and she hadn't wanted to bring him around the guests.

But Beau sat in the saddle like he'd been born there, and she admired the way he rode, with Hank acting like he was a big puppy dog, rather than a spirited, although beautiful, gelding.

They weren't racing in, but they were loping at a pretty good pace. A pace designed to overtake her, she assumed, when he slowed up as he reached her side, grinning over at her.

"Is it okay if I ride beside you?"

"Sure," she said, glad her voice sounded rather calm and didn't give away the twinge of excitement that she felt.

Maybe there was a little anticipation there too. Was he going to be spending the evening with her? Them. She meant them. Not just her.

"Did Tobias tell you I was coming?" he asked as Hank slowed down, and their horses clumped along side by side.

"No. He didn't. Did he know?" It wasn't entirely unheard of for Tobias to not spill all the information that he had in his head, and so Claudia couldn't say she was surprised she didn't know. Although, she had a good mind to say something to Tobias. Didn't he know that if Beau was going to be there, she would want to know?

Of course not. She'd gone out of her way to tell everyone that they only sat beside each other in church because there was no other place for her to sit. Why would people think she wanted to be around him? Or wanted to know anything about him? She'd been pretty clear that she didn't.

"I had called a couple of days ago and asked if there was anything I could do to help. Tobias said that you were leading the singing around the campfire and asked if there was an instrument I could play and give you a hand with." He laughed a little. "I guess he assumed I could sing."

"I heard rumors that you could, and I believe I've heard you in church a few times. In fact, I have a pretty vivid memory of you and your mother singing a duet about five years ago. We had just been stopping in to visit the ranch for the day, and of course we went to church. That was...beautiful."

"Oh. Mom and my sisters used to sing all the time, and I think she misses it."

"Your dad didn't?"

"No. He sings, but I guess he doesn't like getting up in front of people."

She supposed she heard that. There were rumors that Ford Hansen used to be a recluse, but he wasn't like that anymore. Although, maybe he'd never gotten comfortable deliberately drawing attention to himself. That made sense.

"I can't blame him. I really don't either. But somehow, I got suckered into doing the music around the campfire."

"Well, now I have someone to do it with."

"You play the guitar too?" she asked, feeling more insecure than she had just a few seconds ago. She didn't play that well, she'd been teaching herself how to play for only six months. She had about seven chords she knew pretty well, enough to do most songs, but she wasn't sure it was enough to have someone play along with her. Especially if they didn't practice.

"Actually, I brought a banjo. I... I admit that I just started learning on Tuesday. After I talked to Tobias and he said that if I had an instrument, I could come help. So... My sister had left her banjo at the house when she moved out, so I called her, got permission, and have been working on it for the last three evenings."

"Well. You're probably about as good as I am on the guitar then," she said. "Only I've been working for six months."

"Well then, you got me beat."

"Why in the world would you do that? I mean, surely the guys have something somewhere else you could give a hand if you really want to help."

"It's what Tobias told me I could do, so that's what I figured I'd work on. Hey, it doesn't hurt me to stretch a little, and maybe the Lord is just saying I need more good music in my life."

"Well, I guess He's kinda beating you over the head with it, if you're all of a sudden pulling out your French horn and learning a new instrument as well."

He laughed, looking like he might be going to say something else, but then he didn't. Instead, he glanced briefly over his shoulder. "Tobias said he'd probably pass us in the tractor, and then he said that I need to hurry if I was expecting to get supper. Are you hungry?"

"No. I figured I wasn't going to make it in time for supper. I typically cook all the meals, along with Alaska, and Mina has been a great help, and Ada pitches in wherever she's needed. But I got everything prepared, and maybe I just figured I can't sing on a full stomach."

"Maybe we can go out for ice cream afterward."

She laughed. "By the time we get home and get our horses taken care of, it's going to be pretty late. I doubt there will be any places open. Not in Sweet Water. You know how country stores seem to close at seven o'clock."

"Yeah. I guess you're right. It's kind of hard to remember that since the sun is just now starting to set."

As he said that, she could hear the tractor behind them.

"Sounds like Tobias is on his way."

"I hope my banjo doesn't fall off. Norma will be pretty upset with me if anything happens to it."

"It's a wonder she didn't take it with her when she got married."

"I don't think they had a whole lot of room in their house, and then the kids started coming, and she just didn't have time. It's fun, but there's other things in her life that are taking precedence over that right now."

"I guess that's what happens when you get married."

"Especially when the kids come."

The breeze blew softly across the prairie grasses, and twilight settled down. She felt comfortable and safe. Sometimes a silence with someone felt awkward, like somebody should be doing something to fill it, but she didn't feel that way with Beau. There weren't a whole lot of people outside of her family that she felt comfortable enough to be in silence with. Silence was...awkward somehow. But with Beau, it felt just right.

"You're not mad at me anymore?" he asked, and he didn't say it in a teasing tone. The kind of tone he might have said it in a week or more ago, back when he was teasing her every time he saw her.

"No. I hate to say that I was mad at you to begin with. I guess I just... I don't know how every time I saw you just brought out the worst in me. Are you still feeling that way? Like you don't like me very much?"

"I never felt that way. Although you're right, I did seem to show my worst side every time I saw you. I regret that, and I know we've already been through that, but I just want to make sure you weren't mad at me about the bet or anything else. I got teased a little bit because you sat with me in church, and I figured you probably did too."

"Yeah. My family teased me, but it blew over. I mean, I did tell Lucas that I was going to be planning his wedding and inviting everyone to it, only I would tell him it was mine. So he'd end up at the church by himself. But otherwise, I don't think anybody was getting any shotguns and going hunting."

He laughed. "I did nothing to deserve a shotgun. I mean, come on, I didn't even hold your hand."

"I know. You likely missed a golden opportunity to really give the town something to talk about."

"Is that what we're trying to do?"

"No. Not me. I am very happy staying out of the gossip mill."

"Same."

"So why are you here anyway?" She finally asked the question that had been sitting in the forefront of her head since she saw him and he said he had asked if he could help. It just seemed so odd.

"A neighbor can't help a neighbor?"

"When that help involves a banjo and a Friday night working when you could be taking a pretty girl out on the town, yeah. It's a little suspect."

"I don't recall the last time I had a Friday night date, and as for this involving the banjo, I'm kinda glad I got inspired to try to learn to play it. It's not that hard, and I've been enjoying it. I probably should have done it sooner."

"So that doesn't really answer my question." Although she liked the idea that he didn't mind playing the banjo at all. That he enjoyed learning. She felt that way, too. Once a person could read music, there were a lot of things that they could teach themselves. People just didn't want to take the time, because they were too busy...watching TV or something, she supposed.

"Your question. Yeah, I was trying to change the subject."

"You don't want to tell me why you're here? Are you a foreign spy?"

"That's a little dramatic, don't you think?" he asked, laughing.

"It would be something I wouldn't want to tell anyone, and that would explain why you didn't want to say anything."

"I suppose it would, but no. I... I guess I just wanted to help, and your family is kind of compelling. Although I love working on my own ranch, and I don't mind being alone."

"I guess people really are kind of drawn to our family. It's unusual and...makes me sad that my parents aren't here to see it, because they really set this up. You know? They raised us to get along and work together, and they made that crazy choice to have twelve kids. I just, I just feel bad that they're missing it."

"What makes you think they are?" he asked, and his voice sounded reasonable.

The campfire came into view at the edge of the horizon, shining bright in a world that was darkening.

She could see shadows milling around it as smoke drifted up into the sky. Caleb and Lucas had really got things going.

"Maybe because they're dead?"

"You don't think people in heaven can see us?"

"I don't know. Sometimes I wish they could. Sometimes I want to talk to them. I typically don't. There doesn't seem to be any point. And plus, God clearly commands us not to pray to anyone but Him. So I don't. That would be wrong. And even if they are in heaven, even if they are watching, they can't help me anymore, you know?"

"Yeah. I guess. It just really seems sad. I'm sorry."

"No problem."

"I'm here because of you."

He said that studiously casually, and she almost missed it. She had been keeping an eye on the campfire and watching the folks as they walked around it. The smell of hot dogs and mountain pies drifted over on the air, and it brought back happy memories.

Sometimes in the summer, that would be their supper. They'd make a campfire in the yard and cook hot dogs, which, looking back, was probably an inexpensive way to feed twelve children. Hot dogs always tasted a little better when they were cooked over the open flame by a stick that a person found themselves.

And of course, mountain pies, which were just glorified sandwiches, always tasted better outside.

"Because of me?" She turned her head and looked at him, her brows drawing down.

"Is that so hard to believe?"

"Because you hate me and are trying to get information on me that will enable you to...I don't know, tease me more?"

"Probably the opposite," he said, in that same, casual tone that he used to drop the bomb in the first place.

He was there because of her. And it was the opposite of gathering information because he hated her.

So that meant...he liked her?

"So are you saying that the people who are planning our wedding are smart?"

"I'm not going to make any judgment calls on the intelligence of anyone who will plan a wedding for someone they don't know or who aren't privy to the personal lives of the people that they plan to plan the wedding for."

That sounded a little bit more like him, with a little bit of humor and a twinkle in his eye.

They were close enough to the campfire that she thought they better not talk about that anymore. She didn't know what to say, what questions to ask to figure out exactly what he meant.

Maybe he meant it that way too. To just keep her guessing, so she was off balance.

Although why he would want to do that, she had no idea. But the fact remained that she didn't really trust him. He admitted to making a bet about her, had teased her every chance he got, and had only recently started being nice to her. It just seemed...weird.

"On the way here, I felt like I should spend the time asking you what songs you were going to be playing and trying to figure out whether or not I knew the chords for them. I guess we'll just wing it."

"It'll feel very campy if it's not perfect."

That wasn't what she wanted to talk about, but it probably would have been a better topic of conversation than what they had ended up discussing.

That had just gotten her discombobulated to the point where she couldn't even remember the songs that she had been planning on playing.

"All I know is that we really can't take requests, because I have no idea how to play more than a dozen or so songs."

"Or we'll just have to sing them without music. We can do that. In fact, the guitar and banjo are probably luxuries. If I can't play it, I'll sing it, and if I don't know how to sing it, I'll, I don't know, do some kind of weird rhythmic beat."

"Well. All right, so if I think I hear some kind of bomb ticking away, it's just you being weird and rhythmic."

"Yeah. So, don't worry about any explosions. Just focus on your music."

"You are not reassuring me."

He grinned at her, and they made it to the circle where the horses that had pulled the wagons out were tied, so they stopped their own mounts and dismounted.

At the very least, Beau's appearance had made her day much more interesting, if not more stressful. She supposed, when she got time, maybe tomorrow morning when she had a day off, she'd relax in the lake, and maybe she'd think about what he said. It shouldn't affect her, but there had been some kind of weird attraction that she felt for him for a while. Having him say that he was here just for her made her think that maybe she wasn't the only one.

It also made her wonder what in the world they were going to do about it.

Chapter Fifteen

"Hey there, Mina," Beau said, holding a cup of coffee and smiling at the young girl as she came over.

He'd been watching Claudia as she mingled with the guests, smiling and laughing and just making people feel at home.

He wished he had that natural charm that put people at ease immediately, but he just didn't. He never knew what to say, and when he forced himself to say something, it was always the wrong thing. But it was fun to watch Claudia mingle. He admired her and seemed to have a hard time moving his eyes away from her.

Tobias hadn't said too much when Beau asked if he had anything that Beau could do to help out.

It was like Beau might as well have said to Tobias, "I have a big crush on your sister, and I'd really like to spend some time with her, do you think you could throw us together somewhere?'" Short of putting him in the kitchen, Tobias had read exactly what he wanted and given him the absolute best thing that he possibly could have.

He owed Tobias, big time.

"Hey, Mr. Beau. I told Alaska that you had a big crush on Claudia and that you'd be at the ranch before we knew it, and I don't think she believed me. So I can't wait to go home and tell her tonight that I was right."

"Oh really?" he said. He couldn't contain a smile as he looked down at the smug look on Mina's face.

"Really." She nodded her head and then crossed her arms over her chest. "So I'm here to ask what exactly your intentions toward Miss Claudia are?"

"Oh. So, do you want my short-term intentions or my long-term intentions?" Beau asked, just to give himself a little bit of time. He hadn't been expecting to be grilled on his feelings toward Claudia and what exactly he intended to do about them. It really hadn't gotten any further than just spending a little time with her.

"Both."

He shouldn't have given her a choice.

"All right. Tonight, I'd like to sing with her, even though I've only been playing the banjo for three days."

"You're playing the banjo?" she asked, totally forgetting about Claudia. Which hadn't been Beau's intention, but he really liked the fact that he achieved a result he hadn't anticipated.

"For three days. I think you'll be able to tell that when I start to play, but that's what I'm here for, so that's what I'm going to do."

"Well, what do I have to do to get you to teach me to play the banjo? They have one in the house. In fact, they have a whole room full of instruments. One more person could live in the house if they didn't have so many instruments that they take up an entire room."

"Really? So everyone in the family plays an instrument?" he asked, although he didn't quite believe it. Where did you find a family where everyone played an instrument? Unless of course they were on TV somewhere.

"That's what I understand. And I really want to play, but everyone's too busy to teach me."

"You tell me what Miss Claudia is doing tomorrow morning, and I'll set up a time to give you some lessons. Although, did I mention that I've only been playing for three days?"

"That's four more days than I've been playing. I'm not sure I'll be able to borrow a banjo, but I'll ask." Mina's eyes skittered to the side, and she gave a considering look to Claudia who was across the campfire.

"You didn't hear this from me, okay?" Her skinny little arms pushed tight against her chest as she eyed him from under her brows.

"All right. I will never tell."

"You better not, or I'll come get you somewhere."

"All right." He wasn't afraid, not really, but he considered his word his bond, even if it was given to a twelve-year-old who looked like a ten-year-old.

"She's going out on the lake tomorrow. She's getting up early, because she said she loves to see the sunrise from the water. So she's going to take the canoe out on the lake."

"Canoe?"

"Yes. She said so."

"Where's the lake?" There were several lakes around Sweet Water, and there was even one on the northern property line between his family's ranch and Claudia's. But that was too far away from here for Claudia to take an early morning ride. Or so he thought.

"It's one that they have on their property. It's..." Mina scrunched up her face, as though she were trying to think about where they'd said that the lake was. He hoped her memory was good. He didn't know if they had more than one lake on their property and didn't want to go on a wild goose chase at three o'clock in the morning, although he would definitely be up and trying to find the lake at that hour.

Not just because he wanted to spend time with Claudia, but because he was thinking that it was dangerous for her to be on the lake by herself. He hoped she planned on wearing a life jacket. Maybe he'd try to dig some up and take them with him.

Back when he was a kid, he'd more than once gone to the lake to go fishing and kayaking. And swimming of course. He loved every second of it, but it had been years since he'd been on the water.

Watching the sun come up over the water sounded like a fun thing to do, and he smiled a little at the thought that it was something Claudia would enjoy.

Mina turned around and pointed to the road. And she gave him directions that he thought he could follow.

He supposed that he could use his GPS to try to find it too. Surely there weren't multiple lakes in the area that he'd never heard of.

"Thank you. How about we work on your banjo before orchestra? Would you mind?"

"No. If I get good enough, I bet Claudia will give me a part. I know she needed more people, and I'd like to help her out, but...I might not be any good." She looked down a little. And he wondered exactly what her story was that she ended up so far away from her parents, with the Clybourns. Of course, if he had to land somewhere without his parents as a junior high kid, he couldn't really think of a better family than the Clybourns to end up with. But it still didn't negate the fact that a kid wanted to be with her parents and at the very least wanted to know that their parents wanted them.

"I'm sure she will. And at least so far, it hasn't been hard. I haven't had any trouble at all. It hurt my fingers at first, and I bet it will hurt yours even more, but other than that, it's been pretty easy."

"I always heard the banjo was really hard."

"Maybe I just don't know enough to know that it's going to get a lot harder. But the first three days won't be that bad."

"All right. It's a deal. I'll be there before orchestra. I know that Miss Claudia is going to go early because she was going to help some of the kids that were playing. I think the string section she said, all needed help."

"Yeah. I think it is pretty hard to play the violin. Although, I've never tried."

Mina lifted her shoulders, like she had no idea either, and she gave him one last look, a look of they'd made a bargain and she expected him to keep it, before she said, "Good luck with your plan tomorrow."

"Thanks."

He watched her stride away, not mingling with the guests with the poise and maturity that Claudia had, but it was obvious that she'd been watching Claudia and was trying to imitate her a bit. She definitely was good with the kids and had some of them laughing.

There weren't too many, maybe twenty guests total, plus four or five kids.

He supposed if he had a family, this was exactly the type of family activity that would be a lot of fun. An evening out underneath the stars, with someone else providing all the food and entertainment, and all he had to do was make sure that his kids didn't run into the fire and didn't get lost. Tame horses and a taste of a life that they didn't usually get to experience. Yeah, he could see the draw here.

Although, it was definitely getting chilly. Later in the summer, it would stay a little bit warmer all night, but North Dakota didn't have too many nights that were very warm.

Which, in Beau's opinion, at least at this point in his life, just meant lots of snuggling, and he had to say, he certainly wouldn't mind snuggling with Claudia.

Chapter Sixteen

"That wasn't too terrible," Claudia said as she put her guitar in the case and set it on the back of the wagon.

"I think your definition of terrible and mine are slightly different," Beau said, and she couldn't help it, she laughed softly.

The campfire had died down, and the folks were breaking off into families and finding their bedrolls.

There were some couples who didn't have any children, plus three or so couples who had one or two children.

It was a great group, and they had sung enthusiastically, if not beautifully.

"I think they mostly sang loud to drown out our playing," she said, although she thought that maybe that was an optimistic statement.

"I like your optimism," Beau said, confirming her suspicion.

"Is that all you guys have?" Tobias said, coming around and standing beside the back of the wagon.

"Yep. That's it for me." Claudia said, having gathered up the food and loaded it up before she'd gotten her guitar out. Mina had helped, and she'd been great, but she had wanted to stay, and Caleb had said he would keep an eye on her.

Claudia wanted to take her with her to the lake tomorrow, and

Mina had wanted to go, but Alaska had something she needed to do, and she had asked if Mina could go some other time.

Claudia wondered if Alaska knew that maybe Claudia just needed a little bit of time alone. Not that Mina was difficult in any way, she just wasn't used to having anyone dog her footsteps constantly. Mina was great, and she loved her, but she was looking forward to having a couple of hours alone. She didn't typically have things to figure out, but...Beau, she definitely wanted to figure him out.

"All right. I'm gonna head back. I'll keep an eye out for you two to get back, although you know you can call if you have any issues."

"Thanks, Tobias. I'm sure we'll be fine," Beau said.

Maybe there was some kind of communication that passed between the two men, but Claudia wasn't entirely sure. She knew what Tobias meant. A horse could throw a shoe or step in a hole in the dark. They would stick to the road, and they should be fine, but if there were any issues, Tobias would be watching out for them.

She appreciated that and couldn't imagine going through life without having brothers and sisters who cared about her. What would it have been like if she would have lost her parents and lost everyone? Kind of like Mina. Except, Mina had the Clybourns now.

Maybe it wasn't entirely the same, but it had to be a little bit of a security blanket for her.

Of course, they were supposed to turn to the Lord for their security, but Claudia would have thought that if she didn't have a whole lot of security as a child, it might be harder to understand and trust God as a person's heavenly father.

They walked to their horses, where they had simply tied them and loosened the cinches.

It didn't take any time at all to tighten them back up and mount.

Tobias had driven the tractor away, and the noise had faded by the time they started clomping out.

There were still some whispered words around the campfire, and unless she was mistaken, Lucas was telling a story. He was a great storyteller, and if Claudia hadn't been planning on going to the lake in the morning, she might have been tempted to stay and listen to him.

"He really knows how to weave a tale," Beau said as Lucas's voice slowly faded.

"He always has. And he just loves it too. He would entertain people all day long. He's...just born for that role," Claudia said fondly.

"I kind of feel like you might have a favorite."

"I do. Is it terrible?"

"Probably not. I guess I don't have any brothers, and I don't have enough sisters to know what it's like to maybe know some better than others?"

"Yeah. Lucas is right next to me in birth order. He's two years older, and we pretty much grew up together. I probably am closer to him than I am to any of my other siblings, although my sisters and I have gotten closer as we've gotten older. I think, you know, women just have more in common with other women usually. But Lucas and I really understand each other, and we have so many memories in common too."

"I was so much younger than my sisters, I don't even really remember a whole lot about our childhood together. It was just Dad and me. But I wouldn't change that. Because I feel like I'm a lot closer to my dad than I might have been if he'd had more than one son. Although... I like to think that Dad would have made sure that he had a relationship with all of us."

"I'm sure he would have. I've always thought your parents were really fantastic. They remind me a little bit of my parents, although maybe they're a little bit more refined? My parents were very much salt of the earth, work hard from sunrise to sunset kind of people."

"My parents know how to work too, but yeah, maybe they're just a little more the white-collar type. Even though we have a ranch, and they both have worked hard on it, they didn't grow up that way. At least my mom didn't. Dad grew up on a ranch. That's how he had his accident."

"Yeah. I heard about that."

"I guess it's farming. It's kinda hard to be a farmer and not have a certain percentage of your friends who've lost limbs, or loved ones even, in farming accidents. It's just the nature of the beast."

"Yeah. Lots of heavy machinery, plus danger. Even though they try to make it safe, sometimes there are just things you can't make safety regulations for, you know?"

He nodded as they rode along in the darkness. She could see his head moving in the light of the moon and stars.

"I haven't spent a whole lot of time in the city, but it shocked me when I did, how muted the stars are there. I mean I know you read about it everywhere, but when you're actually there, you realize how much gunk is in the air to keep you from seeing what we see out here. Can you imagine growing up without this?"

"I can't. How sad. Yet, millions, maybe billions, of people do."

"I sometimes don't think we realize how blessed we are. We take what we have for granted, and it's true, we work hard for it, but...it's a real blessing to have this."

"Yeah. I agree." She allowed her voice to fade off, thinking that it'd been a while since she'd thought about how grateful she was for what she had. She'd been wrapped up in her ensemble and trying to get the dude ranch started, and in the back of her head, she was always worried about finances. She didn't look at the finances as much as she wanted to, but the last time she had, it had scared her, since the ranch needed to make an awful pile of money over the summer in order to pay their back bills and be ready for winter. She honestly wasn't sure that it was something that was even going to happen.

But beyond all of that, everyone had worries. Whether they were health worries, worries about their family, their children, finances, or whatever it was. Maybe they lost a loved one, and they had that in the back of their mind all the time. As she did. But it was always okay to be grateful. And she realized it had been a while since she had just sat down and thought about all the blessings God had given her.

Maybe she would do that tomorrow morning at the lake. Take the time to try to be a little bit thankful.

She appreciated the fact that Beau had pointed her in that direction without making her feel bad for having neglected that area of her life, or lecturing her about how important it was, or telling her that she needed to do it. He hadn't judged, hadn't lectured, hadn't done anything except nudge her a little in the right direction.

It was good to be around someone like that. Someone who made her better.

They didn't talk a whole lot on the way back to the ranch, and he didn't hang around, trying to talk, or getting her to do something, or waiting for an invitation to come in once they got to the ranch and put their horses away.

He thanked her for letting him play with her, told her he was looking forward to seeing her the next day, and then walked to his pickup and drove away.

She honestly wasn't sure what his deal was, but she knew that she'd gone from dreading seeing him around town to...enjoying his company. That was an unexpected development, but it made her excited to go to the ensemble the next day as she stood on the porch and watched his taillights fade away.

Chapter Seventeen

"Are you sure this is a good idea?" Rhonda said as she held the portable drill that Bernadine had insisted they needed to take to the lake.

"Didn't you do this kind of stuff when you were little?"

"I certainly did not. I was a good girl."

"So was I. And I don't exactly regret that, but...it doesn't hurt to live a little."

"I don't understand how putting a hole in the bottom of someone's boat is living a little," Rhonda said, and she felt superior to Bernadine. She was almost certain that she had the moral high ground here, and she didn't want to lose any of it to Bernadine's twisted logic.

"You are looking at it all wrong," Bernadine said as they crept through the night, toward the old canoe that lay on the shore of the lake.

Bernadine had told Rhonda that she had it on good authority, from Mina, the little girl who was staying at the Clybourns, that Claudia Clybourn would be in this canoe tomorrow morning. Bernadine also said that she was almost certain that Beau Hansen would be in the canoe with her.

"I don't think I'm looking at destruction of property in a wrong light at all," Rhonda said, hesitating as Bernadine held her hand out for the drill.

"Fine. It's all me. You can blame everything on me. But at their wedding, I'm going to be dancing, and you are going to be sitting there wishing that you had had a part in it, instead of trying to talk me out of it."

"What if they drown?"

"They are not going to drown. You see these flotation devices? They will be wearing them. They will be fine. They will just have an adventure together, they'll be in each other's company when something bad happens, they'll get to see themselves at their worst and will get to see their character rise like cream to the top of milk."

Rhonda sighed. Cream and milk and character didn't really all seem like they should go together, and there Bernadine went, talking in circles and making Rhonda feel like wrong wasn't wrong, but it might be right, when she knew wrong was always wrong, even when it felt right. At least... She thought she did.

"Just trust me, okay?" Bernadine said before she pulled the trigger on the drill. Rhonda had to admit she was rather impressed. Around her house, her husband had always done all of the handiwork, and she had no idea how to work a drill. But Bernadine wielded it like it was second nature to her.

Soon she had two small holes in the bottom of the boat. Holes that wouldn't allow water in so fast as to be alarming when they got in, but holes that would eventually allow the entire boat to fill with water.

She blew out a breath. She felt very, very uneasy about this. If something happened, even though she wasn't the one who put the holes in the boat, she would feel guilty about it.

"What if they...drown?"

"Did you not hear me tell you to trust me? I know that this will work. We are being matchmakers, not destructionists."

"Maybe we're both?"

"Fine. Do you want me to patch the holes?" Bernadine asked, propping the hand that held the drill on her waist and waiting for Rhonda's answer.

"How would we do that?" Rhonda scrunched up her face. Wasn't the boat completely worthless now?

"I have duct tape in my car. We can slap that over the holes if it'll make you feel better."

"Will that work?"

"It held my clothes together when I was growing up, and it held our furniture together, too. It even held the bumper to our car for years. Not that you can do that anymore," Bernadine muttered as she looked out over the surface of the lake, which shivered in the moonlight.

Rhonda had never done anything like this after dark. She wouldn't have even thought about it if Bernadine hadn't suggested it. She only went along because... Maybe because she didn't feel like she had done a whole lot in her life, and getting two people together who seemed made for each other was rather a noble cause. Plus, an adventure at night after midnight was new and novel and a little irresistible.

Like sin. Sin was irresistible. She put one toe in, and all of a sudden, she ended up submerged in it.

This should teach her.

"Are we going to stay with Jim tomorrow while Agathe goes to her support group meeting?" Rhonda said as they walked slowly back toward the car. Bernadine was good in the water during their aquatics class but much slower on land. Maybe a bit like a sea turtle. Maybe it wasn't a very complimentary comparison, and Rhonda tried to push that out of her mind, since it seemed to really fit.

"I'll talk to her tomorrow morning and see if she still wants us to. She said last week that he was doing fine, and she thought he'd be okay. Although, even when he doesn't know where he is, he still enjoys sitting in front of the TV set watching his sports channel."

That was pretty much what Rhonda already thought, but maybe it was because it was so dark or so late, or maybe because she was already feeling anxious, she just wanted the noise of talking to calm her.

"I guess I just worry about her. She has so much going on."

"And she has friends like us to help her. Just like we're helping Claudia and Beau, we're helping Agathe. Exact same thing," Bernadine said as they reached her car.

Rhonda wasn't sure she agreed completely with that, but she was feeling less concerned about it. The lake wasn't that big, and they would be wearing life vests. What could possibly go wrong?

Chapter Eighteen

Claudia parked her four-wheeler at the edge of the road, where it ended at the lake.

It was four a.m., at least an hour until sunrise, maybe a little more. This time of year, the days were long, but she arrived in plenty of time to be out on the lake by the time the sun was coming up.

She had packed a few snacks and a couple of drinks, just in case she decided she wanted to stay on the lake for a while and eat. She hadn't had a day off in forever, and it had been even longer since she had some time alone. Although... She had so much trouble last night falling asleep because all she could think about was Beau and how she misjudged him for so long. She supposed that happened quite often with humans; they thought they knew everything there was to know about someone, until they actually spent time with that person and realized they didn't know anything.

"I'm being very presumptuous this morning." A voice came out of the darkness, and she almost dropped her lunch basket.

"My goodness," she said, her hand going to her chest as she took a couple of quick breaths, trying to get her heart rate to slow back down. She recognized that voice. It was the one she'd been dreaming about. "You scared me to death."

"Sorry."

"How did you get here?"

"I parked my four-wheeler over there, off the road a bit, because I didn't want you to be scared when you got here and saw that there was another ATV. I thought maybe you wouldn't want to stay."

"Yeah. I probably would have been a little disconcerted. So I thank you for your consideration, I guess."

"I don't have to stay, but...I have a small confession to make."

"Okay?" Was this where he admitted that the bet was actually legit? Or did he admit that he had been using her for some kind of nefarious reason? Or something even worse?

She steeled herself, trying to convince herself that it wasn't good that he was there, that he was potentially not a friend, but an enemy.

"I found out you were going to be here because of Mina. I got her to tell me what you were doing today so I could...spend some time with you. But I don't have to stay."

She thought over the things that he had done—sent her flowers when her dog died, went to her ensemble, brought more people to it, sat with her at church, and came to play with her last night. He hadn't done anything that would hurt her, and all the things he'd done had...showed that he cared. He even admitted that he'd wanted to be on the ranch, had volunteered to help, because of her.

"Are you asking if you can go out on the boat with me?" she finally said.

"Yeah. I guess. Please."

Had he done all those things, been so nice to her, because he was setting her up for something?

"I am...not going to hurt you or anything. I have references, if that's what you're thinking."

She huffed out a little breath. "No. I know you have a good reputation in town. That's not my concern. I... I'm just not convinced that you've gone from hating me to wanting to spend time with me so quickly."

"Have your feelings changed?"

Wow. That was a good question. Because yes, yes, they had.

Rather than saying that though, because she still just couldn't bring herself to trust him, she said, "I would have packed more food if I'd have realized that you were going to be here. Or more substantial food. I mostly just brought snacks. Fruit and some crackers and cheese."

"Well, I have a fishing rod, although eating it would mean we have to start a fire and cook it."

"Assuming you're going to catch anything."

"Is the lady questioning my manly abilities?" he said as she chuckled.

"No. I would never."

"That's better."

They laughed for a minute, and for the first time, Claudia felt a little awkward. Maybe because...she really wanted to like him. Really wanted to be able to let go and just trust him, but she just wasn't sure. Or maybe she was sure, but it was herself that she didn't trust. After all, all of her older siblings had waited for a really long time to get married, and most of them still weren't.

She wondered how much of that was because of their parents' accident. After all, that really brought home to them how quickly people could be taken in and out of their life. If she were to fall in love, get married, even have children, what if God decided to take her husband? She could end up being alone. And wouldn't she be much better off if she didn't have the opportunity to have that loss?

Plus, they'd all been so focused on the ranch that the idea of getting together with someone wasn't something they really had time for.

Beau came back through the weeds with his fishing rod, and Claudia couldn't believe that she was actually going to do this. Beau Hansen, boating and fishing with her.

She'd been looking forward to having some peace and quiet and time alone this morning but suddenly felt like this was one hundred times better.

She set the picnic basket down, and he helped roll the canoe over.

It was old, had been there since they had bought the farm, and she'd only used it a handful of times.

Taking the life jackets, she handed one to him and put hers on.

Sometimes if there were two of them, they didn't wear life vests, but when she was by herself, she always did.

Normally her dog was with her.

"I miss Ginger," she said softly as she turned and looked toward the canoe. If it were lighter out, she'd probably be able to see hair from the last time she'd been in it. It had been last fall, and she was shedding her summer coat, getting ready for winter and growing her winter coat out.

"She's always been with you?"

"Yeah. She went everywhere I did. And she loved the water, although as she got older, she was more content to just lie in the bottom of the boat."

"Still thinking about another one?"

"Yeah. We have farm dogs, and they're great, but...I just really miss that constant companion, you know?"

"Yeah. I've had dogs like that through the years, but I guess after I lost the last one, I just never wanted to take the time to train another one."

"It does take a lot of time to train them right. And it's not really something you can skimp on."

They didn't say anything more as they pushed the canoe toward the water.

"You go ahead and hop in, I'll push it the rest of the way. That way, only one of us gets wet."

She laughed a little and grabbed the picnic basket, setting it in the front where she usually kept it and getting in and sitting down on the front bench.

He pushed a little more, and then the canoe rocked as he jumped in.

"Well. It's not quite as sturdy as I'm used to, obviously."

"I thought we were going to lose it there for a minute. But I suppose here is better than tipping in the middle of the lake."

"Just depends on how big of a fish I catch."

She laughed. "I suppose it's going to get bigger over the years, and someday I'll be hearing about this whale that you caught out of the lake."

"That's the spirit. I haven't even caught the fish yet, and already it's the size of a whale. You are a great fishing companion."

She shook her head, grinning.

He took the paddles and pushed them slowly out. The surface of the lake shone like glass; typically around dawn, the breeze died off. And it was one of the few times in North Dakota that a person could expect to possibly not have wind.

"It's been years since I've been out on the lake at sunrise. But that and sunset are the best times."

"For fishing or to be on the lake?" she asked.

"To be on the lake. In all honesty, I never catch many fish. I guess I just don't have the patience or skill or whatever it is that makes fish want to eat whatever I have on my hook."

"I could never get stuff to stay on the end of my hook. I'd put it there, but as soon as I threw it, it fell off." She wrinkled up her nose. "Plus, I hated to get my hands all dirty. It was hard to read my book, and then we'd go home and I'd finish my book, and it would smell like fish. Or worms, which was worse."

"But whenever you have yummy fish in your belly, it makes it all worthwhile," he said, like he was telling her a great secret.

"Can I admit that I don't actually like fish?" she asked, uncertainly, because sometimes that admission offended people

"But they're so healthy," he said, and she could hear the humor in his voice.

"I think you just said you don't like fish either," she said slowly.

"Yeah. That's absolutely true. I'm not even sure why I brought a rod, but...maybe it was just for something to do." He chuckled a little. "I know, something to do with my hands, because...I'm a little nervous."

"I make you nervous?" she asked, and that did surprise her. Beau didn't seem like the type of person who would get nervous or admit it.

"Sure. I suppose that's because I care about what do you think. And I don't want to do anything stupid that's going to make you think I'm an idiot."

"Well, don't we all do stupid stuff at times?"

"Yeah. But I want to give a good first impression, you know?"

"I think the time for first impressions was like, you know, five years ago."

"This is our first, okay, it's not exactly a date, because I didn't ask you and you didn't agree, I just kind of showed up and crashed your day off."

"I really don't think I'm going to mind," she said, which was an understatement, because she didn't mind at all.

"That's good to know. Because I know sometimes days off don't come very often on the ranch."

"That's true, they don't."

"But I guess it's the first time that you and I are alone together, and I want to...not necessarily impress you exactly but, you know, not say anything stupid, maybe actually have a few intelligent things to say, and hope you have a good time. I want you to, yeah, want to spend more time with me. It's a lot of pressure."

"Oh. So you're saying that you like me, and you think I haven't decided whether or not I like you yet?" She supposed she shouldn't have said that. Those were the kinds of things that people left unsaid, but it just seemed like it made more sense to talk about things and call them what they were, instead of pretending that they weren't anything.

"Yeah. I guess. I guess I should have said it plainly like that, but I was trying to say it in the least embarrassing way. Yeah, I like you. I like you a lot more than I thought I was going to, and I actually did think I was going to like you." He paused, then huffed out a laugh. "I guess I can stop worrying about saying something stupid, because that was about as dumb as it could get."

"It wasn't dumb. But you do sound a little nervous, which I find... intriguing. I don't typically make people nervous. That's new for me."

"I don't usually get nervous, but like I told you, I care. So I guess that changes things."

She wasn't sure what to say about that. She liked him too, but she wasn't sure she trusted him enough to tell him that, although there was a part of her that wanted to do something, anything, to keep him from being nervous.

"Hey, there's the sun." She pointed over to the eastern horizon, where the first rays of sunlight came up over the far horizon. The sky was just starting to get light, and an orange glow seemed to grow steadily brighter, without being obvious about changing at all.

"It always fascinates me the way the sunrise constantly changes but doesn't seem to, and yet everything keeps getting lighter, and you just don't notice unless you're looking for it, and even then, sometimes you don't see it, but it happens."

"Yeah. Me too."

They were both quiet for a little bit, and then Claudia realized that...her feet were getting cold. As soon as she realized that, she realized they were wet.

"Uh oh."

"That's about the worst word you can hear on a date. What's going on?"

"I think there's a leak in the boat. Are your feet wet?"

"No. I have my boots on." He shifted, and his phone light switched on. He pointed it down. "Uh oh."

Just the way he said it made her laugh, like he was imitating her.

"I suppose I should paddle toward shore."

"Yeah. I will try to bail us out, but as much water is in there, I think we'll end up bailing as much as we take, so yeah, let's just head for the nearest landing."

They had drifted out close to the middle of the lake, and Claudia couldn't believe she hadn't noticed that the boat was leaking before.

Maybe it was because of her own nervousness with Beau, or maybe because of enjoying the sunrise. Even now, she didn't really feel scared, she just felt a little disappointed that they wouldn't have a boat ride, a picnic, and the sunrise to enjoy.

There was a crack, muted a little by the water, and suddenly, it was no longer a small trickle that came in but a big gush.

"I think that the bottom of the boat must've given away or something," she murmured. "I'm pretty sure we're not going to make it to the shore."

"Well, then I guess we're going to depend on my fishing abilities for lunch, since we're not going to get that basket to shore without it getting wet. Except, I'm pretty sure we're going to lose my rod too."

"I hope it wasn't an expensive one."

"Not unless antique fishing rods are expensive. It was one my dad used when he was a kid. Actually, I don't even know if it works anymore."

"Well, it's kind of nice that we're not losing anything valuable, although I was kind of partial to that basket."

"It might be kind of hard to find scuba gear in North Dakota, but we could order some in and scour the bottom of the lake to find it, eventually. Or I could try to save it. But if I'm going to do that, I'd better lose my boots." He already had his feet propped up on the bench beside him, since the water was almost halfway there, and he started untying them.

"I bet those boots are a lot more expensive than the picnic basket. Although, I think you probably should take them off. But you might be able to salvage them."

"They were my insulated pair. I haven't gotten my summer boots out yet."

"Yeah. Save them. Ditch the picnic basket. Hopefully these life jackets aren't as ancient as they look, and if they are, hopefully they have enough life to get us to shore."

She had been watching the water come up, wondering how soon they should bail. They could just wait until the boat disappeared beneath them and then start swimming.

"So, I've never done this before. Do you jump out of the boat before it's actually submerged, or do you wait until it disappears before you start heading toward shore?"

"I'm not sure. To be honest, I've never been in this situation before either. I'm pretty sure, though, the protocol is women and children in the lifeboats first."

"Oh, yay. There's a lifeboat. Would you mind directing me to it?"

They laughed together, and he said, "Seriously, I'm going to try to save my boots, but if these life vests don't work, I'm going to let them go and my focus is going to be on you. Actually, maybe we could break off a few boards and use them to help us float."

He shifted, looking around as though there might be a loose board that they hadn't noticed up until that point.

"I think all the loose boards are on the bottom," Claudia said with not a little bit of irony in her voice. "But whatever I replace my picnic basket with, I'm going to get one that can double as a flotation device."

"I suppose when I replace my dad's fishing rod, I should get one that does the same."

"Well, now that our plans for the future are made, is it time to bail?" she asked, looking around. It had been maybe a minute since they'd noticed the water coming in, and she had her feet propped up as high as they'd go on the sides of the canoe. The water lapped at the bottom of her seat board.

"I suppose this isn't the best time to point it out, but the sunrise has really gotten pretty," Beau said, climbing up on his knees so he knelt on his seat.

"You're right. Wow," she said, looking over the horizon. She kind of forgot about the sunrise but realized that gradually they'd begun to be able to see. Orange reflected off the water, and if the boat wasn't sinking, it would have been really pretty. Actually, even though the boat was sinking, it was still pretty, she just wasn't able to relax and enjoy it quite like she would have been able to if she had not been contemplating an early morning swim.

"You gonna go first?" he asked.

"You know something about the man-eating fish in this lake that I don't?" she asked, eyeing the water and really not wanting to get wet. It was probably pretty cold.

"I can't believe that you would even suggest such a thing," he said, not sounding the slightest bit offended but laughing instead.

"Well, two weeks ago, I would have thought you were getting rid of me on purpose, but—"

"I promise. I haven't murdered anyone in a long time. I wasn't planning on starting up any bad habits again with you."

"I had other plans for you."

The first little bit of water lapped across her seat, and she figured that was her signal to jump into the lake. So, at the last second deciding to leave the picnic basket behind, she hopped off her seat and landed with a splash in the lake.

She had been right. The water was freezing.

Chapter Nineteen

"Whew! This is freezing." That was the first thing Beau said when his brain allowed his mouth to start working. He hadn't jumped in to the point where his head went under, thankfully. It had been a long time since he had been a kid, swimming in the water, and this was a lot colder than what he remembered, although growing up in North Dakota, he really didn't know what it was like to swim in water that wasn't freezing cold. Even in the summer, the lakes in North Dakota didn't get super warm.

"Are you okay?" He looked over at Claudia, who seemed to be struggling.

"I think the strap on my life vest was frayed or something, and it broke. I think I can use it, it's just...not gonna work the way it's supposed to."

He dropped his boots. He'd been thinking he was going to save them, but it was more important to him that Claudia make it to shore, of course.

He kicked his stocking feet, pushing himself over beside her. "Let me see," he said, pushing her fingers away as she tried to grab hold of both ends of her strap herself.

He really hadn't used life vests much. The little bit of fishing that he'd done had usually been from the side of a lake. He and his dad had gone fishing occasionally, but only occasionally, but that had been years ago. The older that he'd gotten, the more he was content to just stay on the ranch and entertain himself there. Taking care of his horses was the closest thing to fun he did. He couldn't think of anything more fun than that. Except now...being with Claudia overshadowed that by far.

"Wow. I'm not even sure we can pull it down, because it keeps wanting to float to the surface." The whole time, he kept kicking his feet, pushing them toward shore. It looked a lot farther away than what he was comfortable with.

Even though it was less than a hundred yards, surely.

Still, it had been a long time since he'd swum even a few feet, and the cold water wasn't going to be helping anything.

"What if you hold onto my back, and I'll start kicking. Maybe my life vest will hold us both up, and if you press against me, yours will stop from coming up over your head."

"All right, but tell me if I'm hindering your movements at all. I don't want both of us to end up stranded in the lake just because of my life vest."

"I can tell you right now, I'm not going to be going to shore without you, so do whatever you have to do in order to hang on. Actually..." He had started to turn around and give her his back, but he thought it would be better to give her his life vest instead.

"No!" she said as she realized what he was going to do. "Please. I'll feel so much better if you just left it on. I promise I won't let go of you."

"I just hate having a life vest when you don't. It feels like I should give you mine. That just seems right."

"I'll feel so much better if you have one, plus, what if I'm not able to get it on? And then we both wouldn't have one. And that would be even worse than me struggling with this one."

"I'll make sure you get it on," he said.

"Please? I promise that I will hold on tight and not let go."

"All right. As long as you promise and you let me know if there's any problems? I'm not going to be able to tell if you're behind me."

"I'll hold on tight. I promise."

He would rather she have a life vest, but he didn't argue with her anymore and instead turned around so she had his back, and he felt her arms around him.

His teeth were already chattering, and he was freezing cold. Having her press against him made it a little bit better, except every time her body moved and the cold water took its place, it felt even worse.

"All right. I'm heading toward shore. I think this is the shortest point."

"Yeah. That's what I was thinking," she said as he started in the direction of the shore, not where they had pushed off from but a little bit toward the side.

"I've always wanted to swim into the sunrise," she said, and he heard her laughter. He liked that she wasn't panicking and could still manage to see the beauty around them. The sunrise was indeed beautiful, and he thought how funny it was that instead of enjoying it from the boat, and it being...almost romantic maybe, they were looking at it from the lake, and while their lives weren't exactly in danger, he would feel much better once they had solid ground under their feet again.

She had taken her shoes off too, just because it seemed like a smarter thing to do, and both of them were going to end up walking back to their ATVs in their stocking feet. Plus, it was going to be a really cold ride home.

The sun definitely would not be up high enough to warm either one of them.

As he continued swimming, he wondered if it might be a good idea for them to start a fire and get warm before they attempted the ride home. It was a good fifteen minutes to her ranch, although they could make it in less time if they went faster. But more speed meant more wind.

He wasn't sure what the best thing to do was, but first things first. Getting to shore was the most important thing at the moment.

"Doing okay?" he asked after about five minutes. It didn't seem like the shore was any closer. He wished he had rowed faster, tried harder to get the boat closer. At the time, he was thinking about saving things like his boots and the picnic basket and wasn't thinking about life vests that were older than the hills and were not going to stay together.

"Yeah. I'm good," she said. Her teeth chattered.

She must have been clamping them together so he wouldn't hear it, but she could hardly talk without unclamping her teeth.

"I'm thinking we need to start a fire along the edge of the shore and get warmed up before we try to make it home."

"If there's anything to start a fire with," she said, and that time, he wasn't able to miss the chattering of her teeth at all.

"Good point." He didn't even have matches. "Maybe we'll use one four-wheeler. You can sit behind me, and I'll block the wind."

"You're just as cold as I am," she said, the chattering of her teeth sounding almost violent behind him.

"No. I'm really not. I'm swimming."

"I'm kicking my feet as hard as I can," she said, and he knew that to be true. He could feel her holding onto him, but she moved at the same time. And she had adjusted the kicking of her feet to coincide with his, so it felt like they were working together, rather than her arbitrarily kicking and him arbitrarily kicking as well.

By the time they reached the shore, he was freezing, shivering, even despite the effort he was putting in to get there, and exhausted.

He tried to find purchase in the mud, pushing and twisting back to try to put an arm underneath her shoulders to help her get her footing too.

That was a mistake that knocked them both off their feet, and they ended up falling.

"Sorry about that," he said as he tried again to get to his feet, waiting until he had managed to get a good hold in the mud before he helped her to her feet.

"I don't really care. Right now, I'm looking forward to a hot shower. And it won't matter how dirty I am when I get in."

"Me too. And I was thinking that it was closer to go to my house than yours. That'll shave at least five minutes off the time it takes to go back."

"All right. I didn't realize we were so close to your property."

"This borders the far corner, which is where the house that I moved into is. It's not much, but it will have hot water, scalding hot, and we'll be able to get out of those cold, wet clothes faster."

"All right. I'm in."

"Actually, we're out," he said as they reached the edge of the lake and started climbing up the bank, which sloped gently, although it was muddy.

"Oh!" she said as she slipped.

He was able to catch her, but then he lost his footing, and they both went down again.

That jarred his elbow and hurt like sixty, but he didn't say anything, stifling the groan that wanted to come out of his mouth.

"I'm so sorry," she said, her teeth chattering with every word.

"It's okay. You owed me."

"Are we keeping score?"

"No. I just wanted you to feel better."

"Oh. Thanks."

They struggled to their feet. She held onto his waist, while his arm was around her shoulders, as they walked through the grass in their stocking feet toward his ATV.

The sun was well up in the sky, although he'd caught glimpses of the sunrise and felt like he'd enjoyed it some. He definitely was thankful that they were alive.

"I'm thankful for the life vest," he said. "That made the swim back to shore a lot easier."

"It definitely did. I... I don't think I could've swum the whole way to shore if I hadn't had a life vest. I've never been a strong swimmer."

"You live in North Dakota. I don't think anyone expects you to be a strong swimmer."

They both laughed, and he figured that was true. He was concerned about her though. Her teeth had stopped shaking a few minutes before. He should know more about hypothermia than what he did, but as much as he would like to say that on a spring day like today she couldn't have an issue with it, he knew that wasn't true. Still, he didn't think the lake was quite that cold, but the ride home was going be torture.

"You try to stay behind me, and I'll block the wind as much as I can," he said, wishing he had a blanket or something in his four-wheeler, but he'd taken all of his winter emergency supplies out in preparation for spring planting.

It still wasn't too late to get a North Dakota blizzard. They could happen at almost any time of the year, and he was pretty sure there was a documented blizzard in every month, but they'd gotten to the point of the year where it made more sense for him to carry around the things that he was going to need to take care of his crops and cattle and use his extra space for that, rather than blankets and batteries and all the stuff he carried around in winter for the just-in-case scenarios.

"What about you?" she asked, and he could barely understand her words because her teeth were chattering again, even worse. He also thought her words might have been slurred just a little. She leaned heavily on him.

"I'm going to be fine. You, on the other hand, need to hold on for another ten minutes. Okay?"

"Of course," she said, and he loved that backbone. That bit of sass that said that she wasn't going to allow a little cold to get her down.

He didn't say much more as he started the ATV and made himself as wide as possible to block as much of the wind as he could.

Her arms were around him, and he put his left hand over top of her arms to try to keep that much more wind away from her.

He was freezing cold himself, but his concern was totally for her. He knew he could handle it. He wasn't so cold that he was starting to get sleepy, and his words were definitely not slurring.

He really loved his house, even though it was kind of old and could use an overhaul inside. He just hadn't cared enough, and he figured if he ever did get married, his wife would either want a new house or want to move somewhere else. They could build a house on the farm if they wanted to, although he was totally content where he was.

In reality, one place on the farm was very much like the next. There were a few spots that were a little different, one where the creek went down through for one, a couple places where there were a few trees together, and of course the lake, which bordered his property on the northeast.

Regardless, home never looked so good. He said over his shoulder, "Are you okay?"

"Yeah," she said, sounding anything but.

"All right. I have a bathroom downstairs, and I'll get the shower running while you get your outside clothes off, and if you need help, I can give you a hand. I...know that doesn't sound the greatest, but I'm concerned about you."

"Don't be. I'll be fine. The idea of a hot shower sounds really amazing."

He was heartened that she was still speaking at least.

Maybe he was making mountains out of molehills, but he did know a few people who had almost died from hypothermia, and he didn't want Claudia to be on that list. Especially since the boat went down twice as fast as it would have if he hadn't been in it. Although, he didn't want to think about what might have happened if she had been alone. Especially if she put on the life vest that broke.

Of course, maybe she'd have been able to hold onto the other life vest and get herself to shore, or maybe... He didn't want to think that she might have succumbed to hypothermia.

He pulled the four-wheeler right next to the porch so she could get off and step right up on the steps.

As it was, he climbed off and helped her, and they went up the stairs together. They were filthy, and his mom probably would have thrown a fit if he would have walked into her house like that, but he didn't care at all. His main concern was getting Claudia in and getting her warm.

He opened the door, and she walked in, her arms wrapped around herself, her teeth clacking together, and he remembered that as long as someone was shivering, they were still okay.

It was whenever they went beyond shivering that a person had to be careful.

Chapter Twenty

Beau led Claudia to the bathroom, which was just a few steps away from the door, and he said, "I'm gonna turn the shower on, get it to a temperature that I know isn't going to scald you, maybe a little bit cooler than necessary, and you can get in. Once that doesn't feel burning hot on you, you can turn the temperature up, but don't do it too fast."

"I know. In case there's any part of me that's numb, hot water could scald me before I realized it." He nodded, and she continued, "Are you getting a shower?"

"I can. I guess I want to hang around and make sure you don't fall down or something."

"I'm cold, not on my deathbed. Go take a shower."

He laughed, because she was bedraggled, shivering, and freezing cold, and yet she was bossing him around. He liked her pluck.

"All right. We're having soup after this though."

"Maybe you can think about throwing some clothes in here for me. Is there anything you have that might work?"

"Glad you thought about it," he said, grinning. Now that would have been a little awkward. And he wasn't trying to make this awkward for her. He liked her, sure, but he didn't want to take advantage of a bad situation, and he definitely didn't want to take advantage of her when she wasn't herself.

Maybe in his younger days, he might have thought about it, but now the idea revolted him. If she didn't want him, she didn't want him. He didn't want to have to resort to trickery, or to taking advantage of her, in order to get what he wanted, which was her.

He wanted her for the long haul, not just a stolen embrace that she would regret when she felt better the next day. Or down the road somewhere.

He thought about that as he went upstairs and took his own shower, throwing his clothes in the hamper and thinking about what he could give her.

He didn't have any of his sister's clothes here or any clothes from his nieces or nephews. Which would be maybe a little bit small for her but might possibly fit better than his. Still, by the time he was out of the shower, he figured he'd get her a pair of long johns and a pair of sweats.

He hadn't put his winter clothes away and probably wouldn't. When he lived at home, his mom often reminded him to put his winter things away and get his summer things out. But it seemed like a lot of work to go through to only spend two or three months in summer clothes. While he might not wear long johns in September, by the end of October, it was almost a guarantee that he'd be in them at least two or three days out of the week.

Her shower was still on when he padded down the steps, carrying the clothes.

She might not even need that many, but he didn't want to take a chance of her getting chilled again.

He couldn't just leave them in a heap outside the bathroom door, so instead, he knocked on it and called out, "Is it okay if I open the door and toss your clothes in?"

"Yeah. And can I just say, I love your hot water."

He laughed. He had deliberately taken a short shower just so they wouldn't run out. He had never run out himself, but when he had been back home with his sisters, there had been a few times where they had taken such long showers that they'd run out of hot water.

He didn't want to chance that with Claudia, wanting her to get warm as thoroughly and quickly as possible and figuring that the shower was probably the second-best thing other than a bath, and since he didn't have a bathtub in the house, a shower was what it was going to be.

He had been living alone for a while, and he was a terrible cook, but he wanted to get something hot on the stove quickly, so he opened up a couple of cans of tomato soup and dumped them in a pot. Hopefully by the time she was out, it would be warm.

He didn't really have anything else, other than some bacon and eggs, and he spent a little bit of time trying to figure out whether bacon and eggs and tomato soup, along with some toast, would be okay together.

For him, he'd rather have too much food than not enough, and he didn't really think that tomato soup was going to cut it for as hungry as he felt.

So he went ahead and heated a skillet, cracking some eggs in a bowl and frying bacon.

"That smells amazing," Claudia said as she padded into the kitchen.

"You look a little cleaner than you did the last time I saw you," he said, looking over his shoulder at her and thinking that maybe she shouldn't look beautiful to him, with her hair plastered to her head and his clothes hanging off her, but she did.

Maybe it was that twinkle in her eye, or the way her lips curved up in a smile. Her cheeks were bright red, and her entire face was pink, giving her a slight lobster-like look. Maybe he would keep that lobster comparison to himself. After all, he already felt bad enough that she had been almost frozen.

Except, it really wasn't his fault.

Although, he should have known better than to just grab the boat and take off in it. He should have checked for leaks.

"When was the last time you used that boat?"

"Last year. I know, we should have checked for leaks, and I never gave it a thought."

"I'm glad you weren't there by yourself."

She stopped, and the smile faded from her face. "I thought of that too. And I agree. I'm really glad you were there."

"Hey, it was my pleasure. An early morning swim under the sunrise is always fun."

"I can't say I've ever done that before. And I think I prefer to watch the sunrise from somewhere dry and relatively warm."

"Hmm. A woman with common sense. Just what I've always been looking for."

She laughed, and he was kind of surprised that the words had even come out of his mouth. He hadn't meant to say all of that. He for sure wanted a woman with common sense. It seemed like sometimes women were more concerned about how they looked, and what they were wearing, and the gossip around town than they were about anything that he thought was important.

He didn't really think that Claudia had that problem, and he highly doubted that she ever would. She just didn't seem like that kind of girl.

"You can sit down. This will be ready here shortly. I wasn't sure whether tomato soup would be enough, so I decided I would cook some bacon and eggs."

"I think you make good decisions after you have an early morning swim," she said, and he chuckled.

"Thanks for not having hysterics. It would have been a lot harder if both of us had been panicking instead of just me."

"Oh, I was panicking, but I must've been able to hide it better than I thought, if you didn't notice."

"I didn't notice at all. I thought you did an excellent job."

"Well, I thought you did an excellent job." She came over and stood beside him, looking over his shoulder as he forked the bacon out of the skillet and then poured the eggs in.

"I guess I should have asked if you wanted your eggs scrambled. It's a little late for that now. Is over easy okay?"

"That's my favorite, maybe after poached. I really do like a good poached egg. And eggs Benedict are good. Actually, I like eggs pretty much any way. Deviled, egg salad. I really like meringue, and egg custard is good."

"I think someone is hungry," he said, turning and grinning at her.

"An early morning swim in freezing cold water will do that to a girl. Just for future reference, in case you want me to eat poison, I'd be happy to right now, as long as it comes disguised as food. And bacon is a really good disguise.”

“All right. Noted. Although I’ll just be honest and say that I have no intention of poisoning you, not today, not ever.”

“All right. And I had no intention of drowning you. Not today, not ever.”

“I guess it *was* your boat. Maybe you should examine your motives a little more, although I guess you accidentally gave yourself the life vest that broke.”

“Yeah. Rookie mistake. Next time, I’ll be a little more careful and make sure that my victim gets the proper life vest.”

“All right. And I will never be riding in a boat in the morning with you again.” He looked back at the stove, figuring that the eggs needed a little bit more time before he flipped them. “I wish I would have thought to leave my boots on the shore. Because I’m bummed they’re at the bottom of the lake right now.”

“I’m sad about that too. I know how hard it is to find a good pair of boots and get them broken in, and all that.”

“I guess you have brothers.”

“I wear boots too.”

Her eyes twinkled up at him, and he laughed. “I’m sure you have. Sorry.”

“It’s okay.” She shrugged like it didn’t mean anything. “Here’s your plate. I grabbed two, unless you don’t want to share that with me.”

“Will this be enough for you?”

“Normally two eggs is more than I can eat, but I’m feeling a little hungrier than normal.”

“Funny, but I am too. I cooked six. I think we’ll be good. And the soup will warm you up faster, even if it isn’t as good as bacon.”

“That’s true.”

She set the plates down for him and then stirred the soup, turning the burner off and pouring half of it in one bowl and half of it in the other.

“This is the weirdest breakfast I’ve ever eaten,” she commented as she carried the bowls to the table, and then went and got silverware.

"I guess if she's complaining, she's okay," Beau teased as he carefully gathered three eggs and set them on a plate.

She pulled the toast out of the toaster, set it beside the eggs, and then went to the refrigerator and pulled out butter.

She knew her way around the kitchen, and he appreciated her help. He wasn't used to cooking for anyone but himself.

"Thanks," he said.

"If I say you're welcome, would you consider that complaining too?"

He laughed at her gentle teasing. He had wondered after he said that if she would get offended. After all, he had picked on her a little too hard before they knew each other well enough, and she felt like he was attacking her, which when she got mad at him, that's what it ended up being.

It had shown him that he wasn't nearly as mature as he liked to think of himself.

They set everything on the table and sat down beside their plates, bowing their heads, and he said a short prayer.

In his heart, he prayed that rather than driving them apart, this would bring them closer together. He supposed that it could have had the opposite effect quite easily. She could've been crying and upset. He could have been angry, especially at the loss of his boots.

But the thought almost made him laugh. The boots didn't matter. They were both home, they were both fine, and as long as she didn't get sick over it, he thought both of them would consider it an experience that they would laugh about for years to come.

Even if they didn't end up together, they would have that shared time, and he was pretty sure it wouldn't be a bad memory.

"You think we ought to cancel your ensemble practice tonight?" he asked.

If she thought it was weird that he said "we," she didn't say anything. He wasn't trying to take it from her, and he wasn't trying to be the co-director. It just slipped out. He didn't know why he seemed to think of that as something that they were doing together, but he did.

"I think it'll be okay. I have to go a little early to get set up, and I told the string section I would work with them before we started. But there's plenty of time. I suppose whenever you take a sunrise swim, the day feels a little longer."

"That will be one benefit. One of a few. But not many."

"No. It could grow on me. At the time, I didn't enjoy it, but maybe I would do it in a slightly shorter distance if I had a choice, and...an indoor pool, with a shower nearby, and proper attire as well."

"You saying you don't like my long johns?"

"I didn't say that, but I think they'd look better on you." She laughed. "Not that I've ever seen you in your long johns."

"Well, that's a relief. I was wondering what in the world you were doing sneaking around my house at night and looking in my windows."

"It was a little bit odd that you gave me your underwear to wear. I mean, come on, is this really all you have?"

"I couldn't think of anything better. My sweats are baggy on me, but the long underwear is pretty much skintight, so I figured it would be less droopy on you."

"Actually, I used a rubber band to pull the waist together and keep it up."

"I see. Well, she's resourceful anyway."

"Sure. I took you along so you could drag me out of the lake. I'd say that's resourceful."

He was quiet for a moment, because her comment had reminded him that if he hadn't been there, things could have ended quite differently for her. He knew that there was no point thinking along those lines. That God had everything under control, and that he didn't need to worry about it, but it was still a thought that would probably wake him up for many nights to come.

They chatted through breakfast about nothing in particular and did the dishes together.

"I hate to take you home like that, but I didn't think to throw your clothes in the washer."

"It's okay. There probably won't be too many people around the house anyway."

She turned toward him, and he was standing so close her shoulder bumped into his chest. She put a hand out to steady herself, and before he could think about it, he put a hand over top of her hand, to keep it there.

"I had a good time. I know it...didn't quite go the way we planned, but...I guess I kind of feel like anything I do with you is going to be fun."

"That's funny, I was just turning to tell you the exact same thing. I wasn't sure whether I could trust you. I felt like maybe you were just setting me up to pull the rug out from underneath me."

"I promise it's not true. I truly—"

"No. I was going to say that I know that that's not true. And I actually knew it for a while, I just, I guess after so long of us being antagonistic toward each other, it was hard for me to let go of that and embrace the idea that I liked you. I did. But the idea of telling you was kind of scary. Because I thought I couldn't really trust you enough to trust you with my feelings."

"I see. And...that's changed?"

"Yeah. That suddenly changed. I guess if I can trust you to drag me out of the lake, trust you to get me home, trust you to make sure I got warmed up and got dressed and fed and that I was okay...I can trust you to take care of my tender feelings."

<h1 style="text-align:center;font-style:italic">Chapter Twenty-One</h1>

Beau wasn't sure what to say. Claudia trusted him. That was a huge thing. He hadn't even thought that that might be the issue. That she might have the same feelings that he did but just not be able to say what they were. To trust that he would be okay and not hurt her. That made him sad, in a way, but obviously, she'd gotten over that. It was a reputation that he knew he deserved from her, but that hopefully he'd changed. Or she'd just seen that he wasn't the person he showed himself to be before.

His fingers wrapped around hers, and somehow they ended up threaded together, and his other hand went around her, pulling her closer.

He had said to himself that he wasn't going to take advantage of her, wasn't going to do anything that might be considered inappropriate, as long as she was recovering at his house. That wasn't why he brought her here, except he found himself wanting to bend closer.

"I guess since the first time I saw you, there was something about you that was different from every other girl. I think that's why I teased you so hard. Maybe it was because I wanted to push you away, because... this is a little bit scary to me. I'm not used to...I guess you said trusting me. That you trusted me. I trust my parents. And I have a few friends that I trust as well, but trusting a woman... I don't know. Not that I have anything against women, it's just maybe feelings. You're right. They're tender."

He did not explain what he wanted to say, and he was really messing up.

"I guess I pushed you away because I was scared. That's the bottom line. And it doesn't sound very good, and I'm embarrassed and ashamed, but it's pretty much the truth."

"I suppose I was scared as well. I have to say, I felt the same way about you. Like there was something different about you. And maybe now, looking back, it was just the Lord showing me that you were different, but I don't know, after losing my parents, I just know firsthand how the pain that losing someone feels. You know?"

"The pain of losing someone you're close to?"

"Yeah. Someone that you love with all your heart, someone that you never thought you would have to live without, someone you miss on a daily basis even ten years later, because my mom isn't there for me to talk to about this. Maybe she would have been able to help me see far earlier than I was able to that you are a good guy."

"I'm glad you think that. I hope that's true."

"I know it is. I talk to my sisters, but it's not the same? Sometimes you just want your mom."

"I wish I could do something about that."

"I wasn't looking for pity. I promise. I was just trying to explain why this is so scary for me. Maybe it's part of the reason that a lot of my siblings never got married. It's that losing someone is hard. And so you want to be really careful who you give your heart to, because you know that you're not just trusting them to take care of it, but you're risking the fact that they might not be around. They might leave. Through no fault of their own, just... God might take them away. And I know... I know God does things for reasons, and I know that I'm a better person for going through what I did, it was just...hard. And hurtful. I really don't ever want to do it again."

She hung her head a little, and he got the feeling that she was a little bit ashamed. Like she didn't want to admit it, or like she knew that she should be braver or trust God more.

"So...can I kiss you? I mean, you don't have to marry me on the spot, and it doesn't have to mean anything more than what you wanted it to, but...it's pretty much all I can think about right now, other than how I wish there were some other way for me to comfort you. I know that that's not the best way, but...I want to."

Her eyes had widened, but then her familiar smile curved up her lips. "It might not be comfort, but I can pretty much guarantee it'll take my mind off everything else."

"Wow. That's quite a compliment, when I haven't even tried to kiss you yet. You've got a lot of faith in my abilities."

"Maybe I just have a lot of faith in mine," she said with a cheeky grin, which he absolutely loved. He hadn't realized there was so much pain under the surface of her smiles and her laughter and her generally positive attitude. It had surprised him how deeply she felt about her mom and her death and all of the things that she had just said, and he was impressed at how she pushed it aside day after day and continued on with the business of living. She could be morose all the time and end up making everyone else around her miserable. But she didn't.

And she had said he could kiss her. It really didn't get much better than that. Not in his book.

He lowered his head, and she lifted hers, and they were both kind of smiling as their teeth met before their lips did.

He lifted his head a little. "All right. I think we could use a little practice on that."

"You mean coming in for the landing? Yeah. That was a little bumpy."

She wasn't supposed to think kissing him was funny. "I've never kissed a girl and then been compared to an airplane."

"Oh. And now he's going to bring the other girls that he's kissed into this relationship, such as it is. Go ahead, I'm listening."

He probably would have to talk about that. He wouldn't want her to meet someone in town that he used to be in a relationship with and for Claudia to not know it. It might have been different if she didn't end up with him, but anyone he'd kissed would have the upper hand with her, not that it was a competition, and not that there were that many.

"So, do you want me to start with first grade?"

"You kissed someone in first grade?" she said in disbelief.

"Is that not normal?" he said hesitantly.

"No? First grade, for goodness' sake. Why in the world were you kissing someone?"

"Because one of my buddies dared me."

"Oh my goodness. Wow. You are really susceptible to peer pressure, do you know that?"

"I like to think that I've gotten a little better at that over the years. But you're probably right." He thought about the bet that he had with Gordon, and he figured she was probably thinking about it too. "I promise, no one has dared me to kiss you. I really want to. But the girl that I kissed in first grade, her name was Jill, was not someone I wanted to kiss. At best, the whole reason my buddy dared me to do it was because I had said I never would."

"Well. So you kissing a girl is not contingent on you liking a girl. Interesting. I'm learning a lot about you right now."

He could kick himself. He totally ruined the mood. Why did he have to go and bring up any other girl in the middle of lowering his head to kiss her?

It was like he was twelve instead of thirty.

"Have you ever wanted to get a do-over?" he asked, his hand moving gently over her upper back, as he thought about all the things he could have done instead of the thing he did.

He should have just lowered his head and kissed her without saying a word.

"Yeah. Like this morning. Instead of getting in the boat, I would check it for holes."

"And when you found a hole, what would you have done?"

"I guess I would ask if you want to sit on the four-wheelers and watch the sunrise together. I suppose, we could have gotten this kissing thing out of the way then, instead of...waiting until now, when you're currently in the mood to talk about all of your other girlfriends."

"Man. I'm never gonna live that down, am I?"

"No. I'm sorry. You're just not."

"Can't we talk about your boyfriends?"

"We would have a very short conversation about that. There was one, he was kind of serious, but he left for college and I stayed home, and he found a girlfriend on campus. And then, I had one in my twenties. We decided to move, he decided he didn't want to. And that was the end of it."

"So you kissed him?"

"Multiple times. And I guess it was okay, but...I kinda wish I wouldn't have. You know, it just makes me feel icky now."

"I see." He liked that last sentence. He didn't want someone he really cared about going around remembering some other man's kiss with fondness. He didn't want to compete with someone who was just a memory. In his experience, it was impossible.

That was probably the way she felt, and he had just ruined everything, because he brought his own girlfriends up and into the conversation, and he had a few more than what she did. He could still count them on one hand, but he wasn't looking forward to talking about them. And he could say that there was something to be said about waiting until the right one came along.

"Maybe I shouldn't kiss you," he murmured as he thought about that.

"Yeah. Maybe you shouldn't," she said, although she sounded a little disappointed. "Are you thinking in case this doesn't last, and you end up having one more girl to have to explain to the next girl that you're with?"

"How did you know?" He wouldn't have thought that she could read his mind like that.

"Well, I was thinking the same thing. I'm very happy I only have two to talk about, and neither one was earthshaking. I mean, they were nice guys and everything, but I kinda knew even when we first started going out that he really wasn't the one for me. You know you get to a certain age and you're just kind of like what if I don't get married? You know? And then it ended up that we ended up not getting married anyway, and I would have been much happier just waiting on the Lord."

"Yeah. I could say amen and amen."

He sighed, running his hand over her back and thinking about what she had said. He really wanted to kiss her, but she was right. He didn't want to add one more girl to the string of girls that he had kissed and didn't marry. It was like kissing someone else's wife.

Of course, they weren't married at the time, but it was still the idea that he'd taken something that wasn't really his. Kissing wasn't fornication or anything, but it definitely wasn't something he would do with just anyone. Not in this stage of his life. Back when he was younger, he definitely had more of a desire to be physical before he was ready for any kind of serious emotional attachment.

"When I was younger, kissing was more about the physical. It wasn't really that I looked at a woman and saw her character, and admired that, and realized that that was the kind of character that I wanted to have in my life partner. It was more about...just a physical attraction. So, I suppose there were some passionate kisses in my past, but some of those I can't even remember the name of the girl that I was kissing at the time without thinking about it pretty hard. Is that terrible?"

"Yeah. That is pretty terrible, but nice to hear too. I wouldn't really want things between us to go further if you had fond memories of someone that you kissed but was now married to someone else, so now you're just looking for someone to take her place."

"That's not very appealing. But again, you don't have to worry about that. And I suppose, now that we've discussed it, number one, I've never had a kiss be a total flop the way that almost-kiss between us just was, and number two, I've never had anyone that I wanted to kiss more."

He sighed. But he backed away, dropping one hand from her back but keeping a hold of her hand.

"I suppose that means we gotta wait a little. Right?"

She looked down, and then she nodded, and he didn't have any trouble reading that expression. She was almost as disappointed as he was. But he felt that they were making the mature decision and not just running ahead with whatever kind of feelings they were feeling at the time. It felt like an adult thing to do.

They stared at each other for a bit, as though each of them was wondering if the other one was going to cave.

He wanted to kiss her so much his hands were shaking, and he was almost positive that she was exactly the one the Lord wanted him to have, but while they'd known each other for a while, they really had only been on talking terms, as in a conversation, not hurling insults at each other, for a week or two.

"I'm looking for something long-term. I'm not looking for whatever feels good for right now. Just throwing that out there."

"Yeah. I... I want that too. So I guess maybe if this seems like it's going to be long-term, we should talk about that."

"But maybe not today." He huffed out a breath. "It's been quite a day, and while I feel like I'm totally rational, and you seem like you are too, this probably is not a good day to make decisions about the rest of our lives."

"No. And I need a little bit of time to recover from my disappointment."

That made him smile, and he knew his lips curved up and his eyes squinted. "Well, you sure know how to make a guy feel better anyway."

"Hey, it's all about timing. Like, when you're about to kiss someone, you don't bring up all the girls you've ever kissed before. Just, you know, giving you a little bit of a helpful hint there in case the situation ever happens again."

"With you?"

"Or someone else."

"I think I'm happy right here. And I might park here for a while, for forever. But I think I might need to wait a little longer until you come around."

"I'm getting there. Give me some time."

He jerked his head, and he wondered how much time a little bit of time was.

He supposed it didn't matter; if he thought she was the one, he should be willing to wait as long as it took. Even if it took a lot longer than what he wanted it to. How long was that? Weeks? Months? Years? Was he willing to wait years for her?

Forever? Was he willing to wait forever? Did he believe that she was the one for him so strongly that he wouldn't take anyone else, if he couldn't have her?

That was a good question.

And he wasn't entirely sure of the answer.

Chapter Twenty-Two

"So what we're going to try to do is follow the bowings on the music so that we're all bowing in the same direction." Claudia demonstrated, with her viola, as she stood in front of the four students who were in the string section.

They looked at her seriously, and then they looked back at their music as they lifted their instruments.

She counted out a measure, and they all started to play together. By the time they were done, two of them were on an up bow, and two of them were on a down bow.

She gritted her teeth and wondered if it really mattered.

But it did, she knew it did, and even if they never got it, if they quit before they did, she would be remiss if she allowed it to slide. There were some things that didn't have to be exact. Cleaning her house, for instance. It didn't have to be done to a science, where she picked up every speck of dirt and dusted every surface. In fact, she was of the mind that a little bit of dirt was good for the soul. Or at least for the immune system.

But when a person was learning to play an instrument, they had to be a bit more particular.

She opened her mouth and tried again.

She had to admit, it was a little bit difficult to concentrate on the string players in front of her when, over on the other side of the basement, Beau sat with Mina, both of them with banjos on their laps, and him occasionally talking, and then both of them playing.

He had admitted that he and Mina had made a deal, that Mina would tell him where Claudia was going on Saturday if he taught her to play the banjo.

She laughed when she heard, because she knew that he had been playing the banjo for less than a week. And found it funny that for someone who was so new at an instrument, he was already giving lessons.

Of course, there was more to it than that, but it was still hilarious.

Still, her heart turned over as she saw them both laughing over something and then him pointing to the music, and they started again.

As they were playing, his eyes lifted, and they met hers across the room.

She was tempted to look away in a hurry, but she retained eye contact and smiled at him.

She figured it was probably a sappy smile, but she couldn't seem to dredge up any other kind. He was adorable, teaching Mina, laughing with her, and taking his time and giving it to someone that he barely knew, with no compensation. Surely he had other things that he would rather be doing at home. But instead, he was at church, giving banjo lessons and about ready to do ensemble practice with her.

She just couldn't explain how that caused her heart to warm and expand and feel happy and almost reach toward him.

And the fact that she knew he was waiting for her made her feel like she needed to do it now.

But she didn't want to rush this. Didn't want to make a mistake that she would regret, although...she wondered how long he would wait.

A day? A week? Longer? How long?

Actually, maybe she should hold off saying anything, just to see. Not that she wanted to test him, but she didn't want someone who said he was going to wait and then who lost interest after a week or a month.

If that was the case, she would be better off without him.

Something told her that Beau wasn't that kind of man, but she didn't know.

Still, she was smiling again as his cousins came in at four o'clock on the dot.

She tried to make sure the practice didn't last any longer than an hour. She didn't want to exhaust the little kids who came. An hour and a half of practice was a good fit for kids their age.

And she appreciated Gordon and Beau's other cousins. They were actually really good, and they gave her hope that her group might not be the total disaster she had been afraid it would be.

Again, Beau waited until everyone was gone, closing up with her and walking her to the door.

"Thanks for asking your cousins to come. I have to admit I was a little bit nervous that...either they wouldn't be any good or that you actually had something up your sleeve. I mean, after today, I was pretty sure that the idea that you had something up your sleeve was wrong, but it was just nice to know for sure that my fears were completely unfounded."

"Glad you know that now," he said, and he seemed subdued. It worried her that maybe he had already changed his mind, and she'd missed her opportunity.

She tried to tell herself that if he had changed his mind so quickly, it wasn't an opportunity that she had missed, but she had narrowly escaped making a major mistake.

"What's the matter?" she asked.

"Nothing. Really. I guess the idea that I almost lost you today has just set in. That we could have been having a completely different evening than what we just did. You know?"

"But we didn't. And God is in control. There's no point in getting upset about it."

"I know that in my head, but that doesn't really keep me from thinking about it. I know I should change my thinking and focus on something else, but it just nags me. Like...was there any way to prevent that? How do we keep you safe in the future? I guess I'm kind of at the point where I want to follow you around with pillows and a safety net and make sure that nothing happens to you. And that's crazy, isn't it?"

"Yeah. It really is." But she didn't know how to fix it or help him. They were quiet as he walked her to her car and bid her good night, not even joking about any nonexistent kissing.

Chapter Twenty-Three

Beau left the church, and he figured he'd better go talk to his dad. He maybe should have talked to him before this. His dad always said it was a wise idea to discuss a woman with a trusted friend or parent before he got so emotionally involved with her that he wouldn't want to hear the truth and resisted it.

He'd always found that to be wise, especially as he got into his twenties and his thirties. He'd always told himself that he was going to go to his dad and see what his dad said before he made a move. And there he was, he'd almost kissed Claudia, and he was definitely more emotionally involved with her than he should be.

Would he be able to walk away from her if his dad thought she wasn't a good idea?

Even if his dad didn't know her well enough to say, surely he'd shed some wisdom on the situation.

He had a little bit of time before he needed to be at the campfire to help Claudia, so he drove straight to his parents' house.

He didn't knock on the door, but he called out as soon as he walked in. "Hello? You guys still up?"

As his parents got older, they'd gone to bed earlier and earlier, but considering that it was still just 5:30, he didn't think they would be in bed quite this early.

Although the house was still and quiet.

"Beau? Is that you?" his dad called over the railing. They must have been up in his dad's favorite room, the room where they could see the stars. Although, they were probably up there to watch the sunset.

"Yeah."

"I'm up here. Your mom went out to help Tirzah. She...just needs a little bit of help. Come on up. Unless you need me to come down?"

"No. I'll come up."

His dad loved to sit in that room, look at the sky. He had a high-powered telescope, and his parents always laughed that they had fallen in love in that room.

Beau never asked for any more details; he was afraid he didn't want to know. But he'd been brought up loving that room too. They spent a lot of time in it, and his parents had taught him a lot about the stars and planets.

He went in. His dad had already gone back over and sat down in his recliner.

"Go ahead, if your mom's not here, her seat is fair game."

When he and his sisters were children, his parents had spread out beanbags for them. Now, the beanbags were gone and it was just the two recliners again.

It wasn't that his parents were so old, but they'd had kids, they'd raised them, and all their kids had moved out, and there he was. He still hadn't had any children of his own yet at all.

Funny, because he didn't typically go around wishing he had kids, but...the idea didn't seem so terrible right now.

"I kind of wanted to talk to you a little bit, Dad, if you have time."

"I always have time for you, son," his dad said, and Beau knew that was the truth. "I can tell from the look on your face it's about a girl. Claudia?"

He didn't know who his dad's sources were, but they were always really good. It seemed like his dad knew what he had done, even before he did it. It seemed like that when he was a teenager. He'd do something, and his dad would be waiting at home, ready to discipline him for it.

"Someday you're going to have to share your sources with me."

"Just be friends with the older ladies in town. They tell you everything you need to know."

"Then maybe I should be talking to them instead of you."

"Maybe. Because I don't know that I'll be able to give you the advice that you need."

"What advice do you think I need?"

"I don't know."

"Well, what do you think of Claudia?"

"Her character? I think she's solid. I couldn't have picked a better woman for my son, and I hope you two get together. Honestly, I mean that."

"But?" he said, because he knew from the way his dad spoke that there was a problem. He could see it, and he was glad that he had come to talk to his father, because he needed some rational thought on this.

His dad leaned his head back on the recliner, but Beau had a feeling he wasn't looking at the sky. "Well, where I'm at, the problem is she's working as hard as she can with her siblings to make their ranch work. And you've always told me that you wanted to take over this ranch. The way I'm seeing it, the two of you have different dreams. Or maybe the better way to say it is that the two of you have different jobs that the Lord has given you, and I don't see any middle ground there."

He hadn't considered that. "I see. That actually could be a problem."

"Well, the Bible says that a man is supposed to leave his parents and cleave to his wife. So people could make the argument that it's up to the man to go to the woman. I don't necessarily hold to that thought, because if you look in the Bible at examples, Rebecca left her homeland to go to Isaac. He didn't even go after her, he sent his servant. Rachel left her homeland to follow her husband, although that was after Jacob had lived with her father for years. Any woman of David's moved into the palace, although I guess David could be an example but hopefully not one we follow. One woman is way more than enough. Trust me on that."

"I have zero interest in having more than one." Although he hadn't really thought he would go through life without having one.

"So yeah, I think it can go either way. Although of course, the wife is supposed to be submissive, the husband is supposed to love her as he loves himself. So therefore, he wouldn't lord over her, demanding she do something he wouldn't do. After all, he's hardly loving her as he loves himself if he insists that she has to leave her home when he won't."

"I see." He kind of knew that. He'd been taught over the years that a man had a great responsibility as the head of the household, and it wasn't all cherries and roses getting to be the guy in charge. After all, he was the one who answered to the Lord, but even more than that, his command was almost harder, because he had to love his wife as he loved himself and give her honor as the weaker vessel.

He also was commanded to dwell with her according to knowledge, which meant, according to his dad, that he was supposed to learn everything he could about his wife and figure out how she worked, what she wanted, what she needed, and how she felt. Those weren't exactly interests that always came naturally to a man, or easily. And he was expected to know those kinds of things.

He didn't get a pass just because he was a man. Although society often said that, it wasn't in the Bible. A man was actually commanded to know his wife.

Of course, women had their own commands that were difficult to follow, but being a Christian wasn't something that was supposed to be easy. It was supposed to be difficult. They were supposed to be different. And that was part of what made following Jesus the narrow way. It wasn't an easy way, and a lot of people quit.

Or they just made the Bible say what they wanted it to, or they ignored what it actually did say.

"Do you see any way around that?" he asked, hoping that his dad had given him the puzzle but had a solution at the ready.

"You have some options, but I can't tell you what the best way forward is or even if there is a way forward. That's something you're going to have to figure out for yourself through prayer and by talking to Claudia. I don't know how far you guys have progressed in your relationship."

It was a statement that ended a little bit as a question, and Beau was comfortable enough with his dad that he could tell him exactly the truth.

"I almost kissed her today. Actually, I would have, except I'm an idiot." He didn't need to tell his dad he started talking about kissing other girls in the middle of trying to kiss Claudia. That was not a mistake that his dad would think his thirty-year-old son should make.

It was probably a mistake that his dad would find a lot of humor in though. But his goal in life was not to do things that made his dad laugh at him.

"But you realized that you couldn't be serious about her and changed your mind?" his dad said, when Beau fell silent.

"Not exactly. But looking back, maybe it was the Lord just kind of pumping the brakes a little bit so that I can think about these things."

"Possibly."

He leaned back, looking up at the sky, which had started to turn a shade of pale blue. "So what are my options?"

"Well, you could go to her and join her family. Pitch in with everything that they're trying to do. I don't think that you can do both though. So, what you've done here would probably have to either go with you, or I'd have Mitch continue to run the farm until we sold it."

"No. I don't want you to sell it. I love this place."

"I do too, son. But it's just a thing. Just stuff. It's not something we could take to heaven with us, and we can't get so enamored with it that we can't bear to let it go. You know?"

"Yes. I know. I get it. And what's my other choice?"

"You could bring her here. She'd leave her family, and you two would work this place together. You already talked to your mother and me about buying it from us, and we've been working toward that end. But once you're married, we could sit down and have a discussion again about how that would look."

When they talked about it before, his parents said they wanted to live there until they died. And Beau had said that's exactly what he wanted too.

They hadn't really planned out a way for that to be, but that was what they were both working toward.

Now...he could bring Claudia, and they could raise horses together.

Which was what he always wanted to do. They raised a few crops, some hay, and some cattle, but his heart was in his horses. And he thought that maybe Claudia was the same. It wasn't something that they talked about, but he could tell from the way she rode, the way she handled her horse, that she really cared about it.

"Any other options?"

"None that I see." He huffed out a laugh though, and then he said, "I guess you could leave both places and start on your own. I'd really hate to see that. I don't particularly want you to leave our place and go work on theirs, but you would at least be close, and that would definitely make me happy. Happier than seeing you leave the area altogether."

He knew that it had been hard for his parents to see both his sisters leave. Even though neither one of them planned to be gone for a long time, sometimes life's plans didn't really work out the way a person wanted them to.

"I see."

"But I think the most important thing is for you to pray about it and try to do what God wants you to do. Sometimes I think He leaves the choice up to us. There's not a right or wrong choice, there's just a choice that He allows us to have, and either way is okay. I don't see any right or wrong in either of these two choices, but I'm not the one God is going to show that to. That's going to have to be you."

It felt like a weighty responsibility, but at the same time, it felt like it was about time that he grew up and took responsibility for his actions. Not that he hadn't been talking to the Lord about his life up until that point, but this had the potential to affect everything they did for the rest of their lives, and he wanted to make a choice that not only benefited him but benefited Claudia as well.

"Is it terrible that I'm thinking about her, and she hasn't said whether she wants to spend the rest of her life with me or not. But in my head, I'm wondering if she doesn't, if I might just spend the rest of my life alone. Waiting on her. Is that a waste?"

His dad was quiet for a bit, and Beau didn't try to fill the silence. He appreciated his dad taking his time to answer thoughtfully.

"I don't think so. Sometimes you just know someone is right, and...

sometimes it takes them a little bit longer to figure it out." He paused. "I would have waited forever for your mom. There would never have been anyone else for me except for her. But I don't think that everyone is like that."

"Maybe I inherited that from you."

"Maybe. It's quite possible. I think that some people are like that, where there's just one, and there won't ever be anyone else. Yeah."

He could see him being a one-woman man. That was exactly how he felt. "I suppose the decision should be mine. I shouldn't say to her, 'I'll just do whatever you want?'"

"If it doesn't matter to you, I don't see why you couldn't."

"But isn't the man supposed to be the head, the leader? Shouldn't I make the decisions? Shouldn't I tell her how it's going to be?"

"You don't have to do that all the time. If it's a decision you don't care about, can you allow her to make it? I think so. Your mom makes decisions all the time. She knows there are things I don't really care about, and I'll support her no matter what she does, and then there are the decisions that I feel like God is saying we need to do something different than what she wants. Not too many, but honestly, the way we make decisions is we talk about them, and both of us typically agree on it. It's not a matter of me being the head so I just boss her around and she has to do whatever I say."

"Yes. I guess as I think back along my life, watching you guys, that's exactly how you guys do it. And I think it's perfect."

"You don't just fall into something like that though. You work at it. It doesn't happen all at once, but it happens as your relationship grows. And there are bound to be bumps along the way."

"Yeah. I suppose it would be naïve for me to think that everything would just be smooth sailing all the time."

"Yeah. Be prepared, there's always going to be a storm."

He laughed without humor, and then they were quiet for a bit. Beau just really wanted his dad to tell him what to do. But, he knew that if he asked his dad to do that, his dad would not. It had been a long time since his dad had just thrown out commands. He'd been much more likely to give Beau choices, and then allow him to make mistakes, often saying that failure was the best teacher.

"If you were me, what would you suggest I do?"

His dad blew out a breath, and then he straightened, shoving his hands in his pockets.

"Well son, you know I'm not much for telling you what you need to do. After all, you're a man, and God isn't going to tell me what you should do. He's going to tell you. And you need to be in touch with Him enough to know what He says."

"I know. I've been praying about it."

"I figured you had, son," his dad said, and then he looked over the far horizon. "I guess I would suggest bringing her here, working with her some. Spending time with her, not on a date."

"I know how you feel about dating."

His dad laughed a little, and then nodded. They'd been over that, where dating might be fun, but it didn't really give a person an idea of what a person was like. It was when they spent time with the person in the real world, working together, interacting with their families and friends together, doing life, with all its irritations and unpredictability, watching how that person handled those things, that's when a person really got an idea of what someone else was like.

"Yeah. So, maybe just spend time with her. Talk to her. Maybe she'd be happy to be away from her family. Maybe she's just looking for an out. You don't know until you ask. While I highly doubt that that's true, it could be, and then you'll save a lot of time and effort, if you can just agree right away that you'll get married and live here. But I suppose that would be the one thing that I would recommend. Are you sure you want to have a serious relationship?"

"I am."

"She's a good woman. I think that's a wise decision for you."

It was good to hear his dad say that, good to know that his dad didn't feel like he was making a bad choice. Of course, Beau already felt like the Lord had opened doors, and he supposed that if they were supposed to continue to move forward, while it might not be easy, there would definitely be a path. God always provided a way, when it was in his will. Just sometimes a person had to work for it.

"Then I guess I'll see when she's available to come over. I'd like for her to meet you and mom anyway. And my sisters if possible."

"That might be a little harder, since they're both busy with their families, but I know your mother and I would love to meet her."

"I'll have to see," he said, and he and his dad grinned at each other.

His dad hadn't really told him anything that he hadn't already known, but it was funny how he felt so much better just having talked to him about it. He didn't want to rush anything, and he definitely didn't want to pressure Claudia, but he did want to see if Claudia felt the same way he did.

Chapter Twenty-Four

There was a time, on earth,
When in the book of heaven,
An old account was standing
For sins yet unforgiven;
My name was at the top
And many things below,
I went unto the Keeper,
And settled long ago.

Long ago, long ago,
Yes, the old account was settled long ago;
And the record's clear today,
For He washed my sins away,
When the old account was settled long ago.

The old account was large,
And growing every day,
For I was always sinning,
And never tried to pay;
But when I looked ahead

And saw such pain and woe,
I said that I would settle,
And settled long ago.

When at the judgment bar
I stand before my King,
And He the book will open,
He cannot find a thing;
Then will my heart be glad,
While tears of joy will flow,
Because I had it settled,
And settled long ago.

O sinner, seek the Lord,
Repent of all your sin;
For thus He has commanded,
If you would enter in;
And then if you should live
A hundred years below,
E'en here you'll not regret it,
You settled long ago.

Long ago, long ago,
Yes, the old account was settled long ago;
And the record's clear today,
For He washed my sins away,
When the old account was settled long ago.

Claudia grinned at Beau as they sang. She didn't figure she'd ever get tired of singing in harmony with him.

As they finished the last chorus, several of the folks around the campfire had learned enough to be singing along. This was a crowd favorite, although most people hadn't heard it until they started doing it around the campfire. By the end of the week, everyone would be singing it.

Mina and Beau had both improved on the banjo and that made Claudia even happier.

Without saying anything more, they went into Sweet Hour of Prayer, and then ended with God Bless America, as was their custom.

By that time the fire had burned down, and folks were getting sleepy.

"Thanks a lot for joining us. Hopefully we'll see a lot of you back here tomorrow night, and Claudia and Mina and I will be around again, singing some old songs, and some new favorites. If you think of any requests between now and then, be sure to let us know. If we know them, we'll work them up for you."

There was some murmuring, and a few more comments before they left the folks at the fire, and put their instruments back in their cases.

Mina had already asked if she could stay. Phoebe would watch her.

Claudia hugged the little girl good night, as she left her banjo in the back of Tobias's wagon.

Claudia lifted a hand at Tobias, who nodded his head, then climbed into the cab of the tractor, moving slowly away in the darkness, the lights blinking.

"You'd think that would get old after a while, but I enjoy it every night," Beau said, as he walked beside Claudia to where their horses were tied, not far away.

"So it's not just me?" she asked, thinking about how she felt good every evening after they were done. It was something they did to entertain the guests, but it wasn't a hardship. She wasn't sure how much of that was Beau, and how much of it was just because she'd always enjoyed singing and making music.

"For sure. I spend every day looking forward to it," he admitted, as they tightened up their cinches and untied their horses.

"It's only been a week, ten days. Maybe it won't be so much fun two months from now." Somehow she thought that wasn't true, but it was a possibility.

He lifted a shoulder in the darkness. "I guess we'll see. But for now, it makes the days go faster knowing I have this to look forward to every evening."

There weren't a whole lot of men who would enjoy spending their evenings sitting around the campfire, singing what many people would consider hokey songs, night after night after night.

Beau was different, in a very good way.

She regretted their almost-kiss. Or maybe, more accurately, she regretted the fact that there hadn't been another opportunity. He'd seemed to make sure of it. Which she knew was wise, but the more time she spent with him, the more she wanted to spend.

"So, is Saturday still your day off?" he asked, after they'd ridden in silence for a little bit. She enjoyed the silence just as much as she enjoyed talking to him. It was never awkward, but it felt natural and right, under the stars, in the darkness, just a comfortable silence that stretched between someone that she couldn't believe she considered her...a good friend.

"It is. I have ensemble in the afternoon of course." She wanted to ask him if he wanted to do something with her, but she closed her mouth just in time. He was the one who had brought the subject up. He must have wanted to know for a reason.

Sure enough, the horses had taken a few more steps, the muted clomps loud in the breezy stillness of the dark night, when he said, "Would you like to spend the day on my ranch?"

She huffed out a laugh, more because she wasn't expecting him to say anything like that, than because she actually thought anything was funny.

"I would love to! I didn't expect an offer like that."

"Maybe you won't think it's such a great offer when you find out that I'm expecting you to work."

"I owe you. After all, you've been coming every night to our campfire, and singing with me. You made it something that I enjoy and look forward to."

And that was the truth. If it were just her, she'd feel the weight of the world on her shoulders, the weight of trying to make sure everyone had a good time and enjoyed what they did, but instead, she just knew they were going to have a good time, because with Beau, it was impossible to do anything else.

"I don't want you to say yes just because you think you owe me," he started.

She put a hand up, and turned in the saddle to look at him. "That's not true. I'm sorry if it came out that way."

"It didn't come out that way, exactly. I just... I want to be clear. I'm inviting you to come, I'd like you to, I really would, and I was planning on working, but I don't want you to feel like you have to. I want you to do it...because you want to."

His voice dropped a little on the last phrase, and it made her feel like it was really important to him that she wanted to. Which made her wonder if maybe she'd been too good at hiding her feelings. She wanted more, a lot more with him, but he had said he wanted to take it slow, and make sure that they knew where things were going before they moved ahead, and so she had been reining her feelings in. The fact that he didn't seem to know that she would jump at the chance to spend time with him, no matter what they were doing, told her that maybe she was doing a little bit too good at keeping her attraction under wraps.

"You had said that you wanted to move forward slowly. That you didn't want to... Kiss me."

She hadn't planned on talking about that, and she couldn't help that her cheeks felt like they were bright red flames in the darkness. "Until we knew for sure where things were going. I've tried to respect that, especially since I agree. But, I don't want you to think that I don't want to be with you. You could've said let's go dig up your grandmother's septic system tomorrow, and I would've jumped on it."

"I see. Well." He swallowed, and it sounded loud in the darkness. She got the idea that he was nervous. "I talked to my dad about us a little bit."

"Oh dear. That's a little scary."

"He thinks you're a great person. He didn't have a bad thing to say about you. But he did see one potential pitfall."

"Interesting. It's always good to get someone's opinion - someone who you respect." But her stomach curled in knots, even as she said the words she knew she should. If his dad saw a pitfall, it must have been pretty bad for him to mention it. She wanted to brush it under the carpet, make it sound like it didn't matter, because she didn't want anything to get in the way of Beau and her being together. She hadn't even realized how strong those feelings were.

"What was the issue?" she asked, even though she didn't want to.

"I thought he had a great point. I've been thinking since I was a kid that I would grow up and take over our ranch. I've been working toward that end. We've slowly shifted the beef production of our ranch toward horses, which aligns with my interests. I wanted to find a way to make the ranch profitable and still do something that I absolutely loved."

"That kind of aligns with me. I've always loved horses, and anytime I get a chance to work with them on a ranch, I'm doing that."

Did his dad think that she wasn't going to be any good with the horses? Did he think that she thought that a ranch had to have beef cattle? They were doing a dude ranch, surely that showed that she wasn't stuck in the way she thought a ranch should be run.

"Yeah. I guess I got off the subject a little bit. Maybe I got ahead of myself a little."

"Okay?" She tried not to sound as confused as she felt. There was definitely a question, a prompt for him to continue.

"Dad said that while I was planning on taking over our ranch, you obviously were needed here. Your whole family came here with the idea that it would take all of you to run a dude ranch. He said, and I had to agree with him, that if you and I got together, it would probably mean one of two things. One of us would have to leave our ranch, and our family, and everything that we had planned to do, to be with the other person, and immerse ourselves in their ranch and family, or, we have to leave Sweet Water altogether, not choosing either one of our families over the other."

She hadn't considered that at all. She felt like a fool, since it was so obvious. The perspective that an outside person could bring showed again how wise it was to get outside counsel, since a person who had their best interests at heart often saw things that they couldn't, were too close to see. And she had definitely been too close to see that.

Beau had been helping them on the dude ranch, and while she had just assumed that he was going to continue, she supposed if pressed, she would have said she expected it.

But, he often came with his jeans dusty from working all day and lines of fatigue on his face, after working on his own ranch.

She appreciated that sacrifice, and had told him that over and over. But she had never thought that with them being together, it might be something that he would have to give up.

"Wow. I think your dad's right. We... There's just no way that we can try to split ourselves in two. Plus, there would be the question of where we would live."

"Yeah. I have my house on my ranch, which of course would provide us a place to live, and it borders your ranch, so we could probably do either place, but... My dad has been depending on me to take over. I'm the only son and my sisters aren't interested."

"Oh. Yeah. And my family depends on me to help out. You're right, we all decided together that we would move here, and pitch in. Running a dude ranch is a big operation, but it would provide enough work for all of us to make a living, and we can still be together."

"Which I love. I love watching your family interact. I love how you get along. And there's just something that... Is so beautiful and different about having everything done by family. I wouldn't want to take that from you, and I wouldn't want to disrupt anything in your family."

"I appreciate that." He'd thought about her. That impressed her. He wanted to be considerate of her family, and that impressed her even more.

"But, with all of that said, I've been trying to figure out how we can figure something out, because while I want to keep my dad happy, and I want to keep the implied promise that I made to him - I want him to be able to depend on me to take over the ranch - I also want to be respectful of your family, and not cause any problems there either. Just to be clear, I want you. I haven't changed my mind." He paused. "It's not just the idea of kissing you. Although, if I'm being honest, I have thought about that a lot this week, but every moment I spend with you just makes me feel like you were made for me. I haven't had anything that has given me any sign that we weren't meant to be together. Maybe you have?"

"No. I'm the same. I... Maybe I've been thinking about kissing a good bit too. Not just kissing in general, but kissing you." Thankful again for the darkness that hid her flaming cheeks, she swallowed and kept talking. "And I admire your character, your willingness to sacrifice, that you love helping other people, and that you're just... Everything I've ever wanted."

It seemed so small. The words just didn't seem like enough to let him know exactly how she felt. But it was the best she could do.

She could see his smile flash in the darkness, and she felt that flash the whole way to her toes.

"All right. Then maybe we can figure something out. In the meantime, I'd like to show you my ranch."

"I'd be honored."

They made arrangements for her to show up in the morning, and then chatted about the ensemble, and had an arbitrary and completely unrelated argument about which ice cream flavor was the best, then lapsed into comfortable silence by the time they rode into the ranch yard, and unsaddled and rubbed down their horses.

"Thanks for allowing me to come," he said, like she had somehow done him a favor by having him come and help her family on the dude ranch.

"Thanks for coming," she said with sincerity.

They stood and looked at each other in the dark, and in her heart she wished he would close the distance between them, and give her the kiss she almost got more than a week ago. But, he just raised his hand, ran a finger down her cheek, and said, "See you in the morning."

She smiled, and nodded, but her throat was too tight to say anything else as he strode away.

They had to figure out a way to make this work. They just had to.

Chapter Twenty-Five

"So...what you think?" Beau asked, shoving one hand in his pocket, as he used the other to run down the sleek neck of one of his breeding stock quarter horses.

"I'm so impressed," Claudia said, her brows going up, words coming out on a puff of air, which made it sound like she truly was impressed.

The butterflies that had been doing a rain dance in his stomach settled just slightly. He had been afraid that she would have looked at his place and found it lacking. They didn't have nearly as much going on as what Claudia and her family did.

Of course, it was by design, since they didn't have a whole lot of help on their ranch, and they just needed it to make enough money to support him. His dad and his mom had money coming in from their investments, and the businesses that they had together. The ranch had always been something that his dad had done in his spare time, enjoying it, sure, but never expecting it to support his family.

That had been Beau's dream.

"I mean, everything seems to be so well organized, and everything is well-kept as well, especially considering you only have the one hired man."

"It is a lot of work for one person, but I enjoy it. Although I'd be lying if I didn't say it gets overwhelming at times."

"I would think so."

"When I'm working cattle, I do need to get some additional help. Usually that's not too hard. Sometimes my sisters come down, and their husbands help out. It's a fun day for them, and a relief from their normal activities."

She nodded, and continued to stroke the noble face, as Copper pushed her muzzle into Claudia's shoulder, demanding attention.

Claudia laughed. "This one has a lot of personality."

"Yeah," he said, laughing a little with her and stroking Copper's neck. "We don't really breed for personality, as much as we do confirmation and speed, but it really gives the horse an edge when they come out with that magnetic appeal that makes people fall in love with them. Copper has that."

"I agree. Does she pass it on to her babies?" she asked, showing interest.

That was all Beau needed to launch into all of the great benefits Copper gave to each of her progeny. About five minutes into his monologue, he thought to look at her face, expecting her to have eyes to have glazed over, or for her to look like she was planning dinner in her head, but she listened attentively, and he smiled. It wasn't often that he found someone as interested in horses as he was.

"So she throws color and personality. That's huge," she said as he finished up.

"It sure is. When you make a video, which is pretty much a given anymore when you're trying to sell the horse, it's always nice to have a horse with a personality so big you can see it through the screen. That's what Copper does for her babies."

They chatted a little bit more as they walked to the barn to muck out a few stalls that were being used. Typically he tried to keep his horses out as much as he could, but he had several that were on stall rest, one with a sprained tendon in his lower right leg, and another that he was keeping an eye on because she was due to foal anytime.

Claudia knew her way around the stable, and he didn't have to explain to her how to muck out a stall. In fact, he felt like she probably did it better than he did. And she didn't seem to mind. Indeed, as they were done, setting their manure forks back, and sweeping up the shavings that had fallen on the floor, she said, "I love doing this kind of work. The dude ranch is fun, and I enjoy cooking, but working around the animals, the physical job where you get to be involved directly in their care, is the best."

He grinned. That was exactly how he felt.

"I have to admit though that while I love that, I really love looking up genetics and pedigrees, and seeing if I can find a perfect match. There's just something challenging about that, something fun about the anticipation, of seeing whether or not what looks good on paper, comes out the way you think it's going to."

"I bet a lot of times it doesn't."

"True. Although, you can get the color genetics down to almost a science, where you can know within two or three options what the color of the babies is going to be."

"That's interesting. I know, for example, in humans that brown eyes are dominant. I assume that horse coloring is the same."

"Yeah. With a few variations, you can breed for color and for conformation as well. Although, a horse with a showy coat color will always grab attention, no matter what their conformation is. Then of course, you want to breed for health also."

"So many things to take into consideration."

"Exactly. It's a challenge, and one that I really enjoy. I...could lose myself in pedigrees."

"I'd love to see it sometime."

"After I'm done exercising the yearlings and working with some of the two-year-olds on basic ground manners, we'll run in for lunch, and I'll show you my office. I've got all of that stuff on my computer. There are programs that help you match things up, but sometimes the computer and I don't see eye to eye."

She laughed. "I hardly ever see eye to eye with my computer."

They had a good time as they worked with the two-year-olds, and while he'd worked with men who knew horses better than Claudia did, he had never worked with anyone who was so in tune with him. He supposed the knowledge of the horses would come in time, but it wasn't every day that he found someone whom he felt so comfortable with.

He got so involved with what they were doing he lost track of time and by the time they had finished up and were on their way over to the house for lunch, his mother had started across the yard.

He felt Claudia stiffen beside him, and his fingers squeezed her hand.

"Hey you two. I wasn't sure what might've happened. Usually Beau is never late for lunch."

"I've noticed that he seems to place a premium on food, Mrs. Hanson," Claudia said, with humor in her voice.

"He sure does, and by the way, please call me Morgan." His mom smiled, and Beau glanced at Claudia.

Her face had slid into a grin as well, and she nodded. "I'll do that, Morgan. Thanks."

"Beau has never brought a woman to the ranch before, so this is kind of new for us, and I might've gone a little overboard on lunch."

"Overboard? I like the sound of that. Normally we have sandwiches, or leftovers." Beau grinned. "Not that I'm complaining. Anything I don't have to cook is perfectly okay with me."

"That was a nice save, son," Morgan said with a laugh. Then her gaze went to Claudia. "I'm so excited you're here. Ford has been reminding me not to pressure you over much, and scare you away. But, this is kind of momentous for us, since it's the first time."

"I like that, and you don't have to worry about scaring me away," Claudia said, and Beau's heart swelled.

His mom could be a little intimidating because she was so beautiful. At least that's what his dad said, and his sisters as well had found that sometimes their beauty put people off. Maybe because he was a man, Beau hadn't seemed to notice that as much, but Claudia did not seem concerned. "I have eleven siblings - six brothers, so it takes a lot to intimidate me."

"Well, good then. I'll have it on the table as soon as you guys wash up and are ready for it."

"I was gonna take her around back, because we're pretty dirty."

"Sounds good, I'll meet you inside," Morgan said, as she gave them one last smile, and then turned around and walked back into the house.

"She's so beautiful," Claudia said softly as she disappeared inside.

"Really? She looks like my mom. Now, the woman that I've been working with all morning, she strikes me as amazingly beautiful."

She grinned up at him, amusement on her face, like she thought he was joking, and he wasn't quite sure how to tell her that he wasn't, not even a little bit. She was beautiful to him.

"I hope you're having a good time. I... Get a little lost in my work, and forget that not everyone loves this as much as I do."

"I love ranching. Your place is different than ours, but the horses make it special. I wish we had more, but it's difficult to do horses and make money with them. You really have to start with good stock, and we're invested in the dude ranch, so that's the direction we're going."

"I understand."

"Thanks so much for inviting me over. I feel... Special that this isn't something you usually do."

"No. I guess I never found someone I wanted to bring out until you. If you ever want to spend your day off here, just know you're always welcome."

"You better not say that if you don't mean it, because I will definitely take you up on it. There isn't anywhere I'd rather be than here with you on my day off."

"Then it's settled? Saturdays from now on you're here."

Her smile widened, and she nodded. He loved that, that she had meant what she said, and agreed immediately. Didn't try to backtrack, or talk her way out of it like she had just been saying it for show or something.

Also, he figured that if they were going to get to know each other they would be spending plenty of time together in order to make that happen. He couldn't wait.

Lunch went well, and his parents seemed enthralled with Claudia. He supposed later he would hear from them, and be able to ask them what they truly thought, but neither one of his parents were the kind of people who pretended to be something they weren't. Plus, he already knew they already knew her from church and town.

He reminded his dad that they would be cutting out early, as he'd been doing the last several Saturdays, so they could make ensemble practice. His dad nodded, and they spent the next few hours in the office, taking care of some paperwork, and looking at the various pedigrees of the horses he owned, and the ones he was thinking of purchasing, and studs he was thinking about breeding his mares to.

Claudia seemed just as enthralled as he was, and they almost didn't get away in time to make it to ensemble practice. As they drove to town, he had a satisfied feeling in his soul, and felt like that day was one of the best days he'd ever had. He felt like it would be unfair to ask Claudia to leave her family and move to his ranch, but after today, if it were possible, it was exactly what he wanted.

Chapter Twenty-Six

"Alright. Sondra, I thought that was a great idea with the social media, so go ahead and get that going, and if you need any help from anyone on the farm to get the pictures or videos you need, we're all willing to pitch in." Ezra looked around the room, and Claudia held back a sigh.

Things were not terrible on the farm, but they'd had a few hiccups, and she knew that Ezra was worried.

She had been doing everything she could, but part of her wondered if it might be more help for her to...leave. Not that she wanted to, and not that she would be going that far, but maybe this was the Lord saying that it was okay. That one less person to pay would be helpful.

Priscilla and Phoebe started to gather up everyone's plates, and Ada and Caleb stood to give them a hand.

Claudia had thought about asking everyone what they thought about her leaving, but she wasn't sure how to phrase it. She didn't want her family to be upset with her.

"Amish Christmas lights, A Picture Book," Rufus said. Claudia looked over to her younger brother. He had his head tilted, as he read the spines of the books Lucas held.

"Toe fungus, A History in Pictures. Bunion Repair for Dummies.

1000 Ways to Cook a Snake, What the Neighbors Dog is Really Thinking, and How to Make Reusable Toilet Paper." Rufus straightened. "Lucas, I didn't even know you read books. Actually, if this is the kind of stuff you pick up, I can understand why you *don't* read."

"Lucas? I didn't even know there were books with those kinds of titles. Where did you find those?" Claudia asked, figuring that Lucas, outgoing and funny, must have picked them up as a practical joke or something.

"I got them from the library in Sweet Water."

"What librarian in their right mind would purchase those books?"

"They might've been donated. I heard a lot of books in Sweet Water library were," Claudia said, wanting to defend Ryland, who was a sweet, if shy and quiet, woman, and did an excellent job of running the library. It was thankless, didn't pay a whole lot, and she hated to see her maligned in any way.

"I'm sure that's it," Lucas said, and he sounded a little defensive.

"You have a thing for the librarian?" Rufus said, bumping his brother with his shoulder.

"No."

"I can't imagine why else you'd be in the library. I certainly can't imagine why you would check out books like that."

"Hey. They sounded interesting."

"Toe fungus?" Rufus said. "Lucas, is there something you're not telling me?"

"No."

"That's a picture book. I can tell you why you picked that up," Caleb said, as he walked by with an arm full of dishes, heading out of the bunkhouse and over to the farmhouse where they'd get washed.

Claudia should be helping, but Lucas holding books was just such an unusual sight that she had a hard time pulling her eyes away. Lucas was two years older than she was, and Rufus was two years younger. She'd been around Lucas all her life, and if he'd ever read a book, she'd missed it.

He was too busy goofing off, doing pranks, and generally being charming and funny. He'd never met a person he didn't want to be best friends with. That was just the way he was, which was sweet and nice, but that kind of personality didn't really lend itself to reading.

"I don't understand why a man can't change. Maybe I decided I like reading, and I just wanted to go to the library and get some books. There's nothing wrong with that, and I don't think you should be making fun of me," Lucas said, as he juggled the books, pulling them closer to his chest and using his arms to hide the spines.

"If you need some good books, I can give you some recommendations. Those would put a lab puppy on speed to sleep."

Claudia shook her head as the two of them walked out. She would believe that Lucas might be interested in the shy and quiet librarian, except she couldn't think of two people with more opposite personalities. She knew the saying about opposites attracting, but she figured there was such a thing as way too opposite.

"You were kind of quiet today," Tobias said, as he walked over, holding a garbage bag and shoving a couple of napkins that he'd picked up off the floor into it.

"I had a couple of things I wanted to talk to everyone about, but I lost my nerve," she said quietly. She could talk to Tobias. He would understand, and he would give her good advice. But she really should wait and talk to everyone.

"Well I'm listening, if you want to talk." Tobias said, then he paused, the plastic bag crinkling his hand. "Is it about Beau?"

"How did you know?"

"I've been watching you guys for the past four weeks, and it seems like you're getting along pretty well. There for a while, I didn't think either one of you liked the other very much at all."

"I would've called him my enemy. But that was just because I didn't know him."

"And he'd probably say the same about you."

"Maybe," she said, shrugging her shoulder. Now it felt like their issues were all her fault, although she knew that Beau would happily shoulder most of the blame. They might even argue about who had been the worst. Which probably said all anyone needed to know about their relationship. He wasn't blaming her for anything, and she wasn't blaming him. That was the kind of person she wanted to be with.

Someone who wasn't afraid to step up and take responsibility. She hoped she was that kind of person too.

"So what's up?" Tobias said, shifting until his hip leaned against the edge of the table. He set the bag he held on the floor, then crossed his arms over his chest like he was preparing to stay for a while. As long as it took.

"Well, before we get serious, more serious than what we already are." She felt like maybe they were already more serious than she would want to be, if she was going to have to decide that she wasn't going to be able to be with him. She kind of cringed at that thought. She was already in too deep, even if they hadn't kissed. Beau had been right about that, she didn't regret waiting, and still didn't, although she would kiss him today if he showed up and wanted to.

"Yeah?" Tobias prompted, and then was quiet, waiting.

"Before we get more serious, I...we need to figure out what it's going to look like if we end up together."

"You mean if you get married?"

"Yeah. Would we live here? Would we live on his ranch? We really can't cycle between the two. He is one of the main people on his ranch. They just have one full-time hired guy, and his dad is depending on Beau to take it over. We can't work part-time on this ranch, part time on his, and... I just don't know what to do."

"You're saying you guys need to either choose to be here, or to be there. But you can't do both?"

"Yeah. That seems like the reasonable thing. I mean, I suppose we could get married, and I could still work for my family and he could still work for his, but... It's not that we're working for different or opposing sides, it's just if were going to ranch together, we'd like to be together."

"That makes sense. So often married couples don't seem to care whether they spend time together or not. I like that you do."

"But there doesn't seem to be a good compromise."

Tobias took a breath, and then he said, "Maybe God moved us to North Dakota, so that you could help Beau on his ranch. Definitely so you could meet him."

"Sometimes I wondered why we ended up moving here. We could have made things work in Wyoming."

"Maybe," Tobias said, noncommittal. He pursed his lips, and didn't say anything for a couple of moments.

Claudia stayed silent, waiting. When Tobias spoke, usually his words were laced with wisdom.

"God always makes a way. Sometimes He nudges us using the circumstances in our lives. Right now, Ezra brought his wife onto the ranch, and so has Asher. Caleb has also. So, when we decided that we would do this as a family, there were twelve of us and now there are fifteen. I suppose if you left, I'm not saying we wouldn't miss you, but it seems like that would help balance things out. We gain some, we lose some."

He grinned a little. "I might not be so cavalier about it if I thought you were moving to a different state, but you're going to be on the ranch next door. Maybe you guys could still come in the evening and help with the singing, like you've been doing. But your homebase would be his ranch."

"Do you think everyone would be upset about that?"

"I wouldn't be," Phoebe said, coming up and putting her arm around Claudia.

"Me either," Priscilla said. Her tone was slightly sadder, more melancholy. Claudia knew she had been under a lot of pressure because of her ex and her kids and the situation there. Claudia didn't know all of the details, but she really didn't need to. To look at Priscilla was to know that things were not going well. Plus, her kids hadn't been around for a while, and Claudia knew it was killing Priscilla not to see them.

"I was thinking about leaving too. I might not do it right this second, but maybe this fall after most of the busy season is over."

Claudia gasped.

"I thought you might need to go back to Wyoming." Tobias's words were calm, steady, and held no surprise.

It was like he had already known what Priscilla was going to say. Had Claudia really been paying so little attention that she didn't even realize Priscilla was thinking about moving back to Wyoming?

She hated to think that that might be true, but it pretty much was. She seemed to be the only one who was surprised.

"I think you need to do what God wants you to do. And I agree that it would be okay for you to leave. Not that I want you to, but if that's what the Lord wants, then you need to do it."

"I appreciate that," Claudia said, squeezing Phoebe's waist. "Part of what my concern is, is that everyone will be upset with me. I don't want that. I also don't want to miss out on anything, but... I know that Beau has basically given his word to his dad that he would help him on his farm, and his dad has been counting on it. Of course, they don't need their ranch to survive, but I don't want him not to be able to keep his word. I'm needed there more than I'm needed here."

"That's another good reason. As much as I hate to see you go, and as much as I hope that you'll still hang out and help a little bit, I think it's pretty obvious what you need to do. But, I still recommend praying about it." Tobias sounded serious, but not the slightest bit upset.

That had been her biggest fear, that her siblings would be angry at her or hurt by her decision.

"I think you'll find that no one's going to be upset about this," Ezra said, as he and Alaska walked up, hand in hand.

"How is it that everyone seems to know exactly what's going on in my life, and I had no clue you knew?" Claudia said, shaking her head at the group that had formed around her.

She loved her siblings. Loved the feeling of safety she had as she stood in the middle of them. But she...was very fond of Beau. And she knew Tobias was right. God was nudging her in that direction.

She needed to step out of her comfort zone, leave her safe place, and trust that God was going to make everything work out. He already had started it, by having her fall for the person who owned the ranch next door to theirs. It wasn't like she was moving to the other side of the country to be with her soulmate. She just had to step onto the ranch next door. It should be easy.

"I don't want to leave you guys. I love you. I feel safe whenever I have my siblings around me."

"Life isn't really about living it to feel safe." Ezra's words sounded wise in the stillness of the room as they settled down, some of her siblings nodding, as they listened to the echo.

"You're right. I... I guess I haven't had to take many risks in my life. I've always had my siblings as a safety net."

"And we're still here. We're not leaving you. We're still a safety net. God gave that to you. I mean, come on, there needs to be some kind of benefit from having eleven siblings. After all the hand-me-down clothes you had to wear, all the years you shared a room, the lack of privacy, the limited amount of time you were allowed to spend in the bathroom, and all the other drawbacks. At least there is one benefit."

"I would say there's a lot more than one, but you're right. Definitely the feeling of safety of having your siblings all around you is one huge benefit of having a big family. Thank you guys. I love you," Claudia said as she looked around the group where all of her siblings, except for Lois the youngest, had gathered around. Lois was off at an internship for the summer, or she was sure she would be there as well.

"And we love you. And we want you to be happy, with the man God has for you. It's ridiculous that so many of us aren't married at our ages. We need to stop that," Phoebe said, with a definite nod.

"How about you practice what you preach there, sis," Ezra said, rubbing Phoebe on her head like she was two instead of thirty-six. It was something an older brother could get away with, and since Ezra was her only older brother, he was the only one who could.

Phoebe wrinkled her nose at him, but to her credit, she didn't stick her tongue out.

Claudia would miss this, but she was almost certain that Beau would make sure that she got back to visit a lot. Maybe they would make sure that they spent Sunday afternoon dinners with her family, since they'd be eating with his family most weekday lunches.

"Are you sure you can live without me?" Claudia said, looking at Ezra, since he typically made the personnel decisions.

"I don't really want to, but, yes. We can most definitely live without you." He did not add that it would be easier to make ends meet if they didn't have to pay her as well, but he didn't have to. She knew it.

Although, she might be getting the cart ahead of the horse. Beau hadn't said anything at all about getting more serious in the last four weeks, and maybe he decided that he didn't like her that way after all.

She needed to say something to him, at some point.

They didn't have any visitors coming to the ranch that week, so she might not see him until Saturday at ensemble practice. She had plenty of things to keep her busy, including the cleaning her sisters had scheduled.

"It sounds like a serious conversation going on in here."

She turned her head to see Beau standing in the doorway. Her smile turned to a gasp as she saw he held a leash, with a dog sitting at his side.

"Hey there, Beau. You missed lunch, but there are leftovers in the house," Ezra said, walking over to shake Beau's hand.

"Thanks. I came to see Claudia. I...have something I thought she might want."

The bunkhouse slowly emptied out, until it was just Claudia and Beau. And the dog that sat beside him.

"You got a dog?" she said, as she moved closer, lifting her brows and waiting until he nodded before she knelt down in front of it.

The tail slowly wagged across the floor as she touched the muzzle and scratched behind his ears.

"I can't tell what kind it is."

"I'm not sure either. Ellen called me. I had asked if she would keep me in mind for a puppy out of her next litter. I asked her to do that when you lost your dog earlier last month. I... I thought that might cheer you up. But I didn't want to get it too soon."

"No. I wasn't ready to begin with, but... I might be now. So is it yours?"

"No. Someone found it along the road near Rockerton, knew that Ellen dealt with dogs, and thought that it might have some herding ancestors, although it's definitely a mixture of a bunch of different things."

"It's pretty," she said, noting the blue patches that reminded her a bit of a blue heeler, although the hair wasn't quite the right length or texture, and it put her more in mind of a terrier, and perhaps husky with the way the tail curled up at the end and the length of its muzzle. That or maybe some German Shepherd.

"If you'd like him, he's yours. I told her I would take him if you didn't want him."

"Oh I don't want him if you do."

"I have to admit that I've fallen a little bit in love with him, but... I told Ellen that I would ask you first."

"I could never take a dog you've fallen in love with."

"Maybe eventually it will be ours? I'd rather you have him for now."

She smiled. Maybe that meant he still felt the same. "Are you sure?"

"I am. Ellen said she's been calling him Stony. The person who brought him had been calling him that, although I'm not sure why. You can change the name if you want to."

When he said the dog's name, his ears perked up. "It seems like he knows it. He had a reaction when you said it."

"Stony?" Beau said, and Stony's tail wagged a little as his ears pricked and he tilted his head up toward Beau.

"I believe you're right."

"Then I think we'll have to keep his name. Since he knows it," Claudia murmured, "Hey, Stony. Do you think you might want to live here?"

He wagged his tail and looked at her, his warm tongue coming out and licking the palm of her hand.

"I think he likes you," Beau said.

"It is really kind of you to think of me."

"I hated that you lost your dog. I never know what to say to those kinds of things. I want to do something, you know? And the only thing I could think of to do was to try to see if I could get you something to replace it, but not right away. It never feels good to do that too fast."

"You have perfect timing. I was actually thinking this week how much I'd love to have a dog again."

"Alright, then. God has perfect timing I guess."

"I guess he does." Her heart warmed. They had just been saying that. That God had perfect timing. Maybe the problems on the ranch were a cue that she needed to move out. To move on. As much as a part of her wanted to stay with her siblings and keep working towards the dream they'd all shared.

Chapter Twenty-Seven

"All right, I think we're ready for our performance tomorrow. Make sure you're here thirty minutes early, so we can get tuned before we go out on stage." Claudia looked around her small group of students. She was proud of how far they'd come in two months, and she was excited about their performance. They would be playing in the park, outside at dusk. Hopefully, a few people would show up to listen, and it would be an encouragement to her performers for all of their hard work.

She had more dreams, huge dreams, lots of ideas that she wanted to implement, but she felt like they needed to show off a little bit of what they'd been learning, to let the town know and maybe get a few more people involved, but also to encourage the students, because performing was always fun.

She chatted with everyone as they munched on cookies and slowly filed out.

Her eyes were always straying to Beau. She hadn't talked to him a whole lot other than their evening songs around the campfire, when the ranch had paying visitors. Which had been sporadic for the last four weeks.

Beau had been busy, because this was the time of year when cattle were being worked and hay was being made and foals were needing worked with and needed that human touch.

She still spent her days off with him; every Saturday they'd spent together. But they'd been busy working, and she hadn't had a chance that felt right to start a hard conversation. She'd been hoping he would bring the subject up, and she wouldn't have to. Because, while she felt like he still felt the same way about her, it still felt like stepping out of her comfort zone to say, hey, by the way, I can just go ahead and move to your ranch so let's get married and do that.

"Miss Claudia?"

She looked down to see Sherie, her flute player.

"Yes?"

"My mom wanted me to be sure that I told you thanks, and I had a question about my music."

"All right. You can tell your mom I said you're welcome, and if you show me your music, I'll see if I can help you."

She spent ten minutes or so going over the tricky place that Sherie was a little bit uncertain about, assuring Sherie that she'd been playing it perfectly in practice, and that she would do perfectly fine the next day.

By the time she was done talking, she could tell Beau had left the room. They had driven to ensemble practice together, and he wouldn't have left without her. But, it was a nice evening out, maybe he'd wanted to go out and get some fresh air.

"All right. I'll see you tomorrow," Sherie said, as she held her folder in one hand and her small flute case in the other, and practically skipped out the door. She was excited about the performance, and Claudia had to smile as she watched her. She remembered being that age, and enjoying what she did, looking forward to performances, and just loving being able to play the music and to play with other musicians. It always made a person better to play with other people.

She tidied up a little, put the lid on the cookies that were left, and took a glance around the room before she walked to the door, and hit the light switches.

She walked out, making sure the door was locked, and cocked her head as she heard male voices coming from behind the church.

She thought she recognized Beau's voice, but she couldn't quite make out what he was saying.

She didn't mean to eavesdrop, but as she got closer to the corner, she could hear someone saying, "And did you ever tell her that you were the one that was funding her ensemble?"

"No. Don't say anything. Not until I tell her.... Just haven't found the right time."

"All right. If I see her, I won't say anything. When I spoke to your dad earlier, he didn't know whether you guys had figured things out or not. But if it's still a secret, then it's safe with me."

Claudia knew she shouldn't be eavesdropping, so she made her feet move, and the men appeared as she came around the corner. A tall man, broad shouldered and thick chested put his hand on Beau's shoulder and clasped it. She assumed that was the man who had asked if someone knew that he was funding the ensemble.

A feeling almost like nausea rose in her chest. Beau? Why hadn't he told her? Why hadn't he just donated to her?

Why had he gone through all the trouble of creating an elaborate scheme where someone else was funneling the money and giving it to her? Why would he want to hide that?

It wasn't that the idea was so terrible, it was the fact that he obviously kept it a secret from her. Why?

"Adrian, here's the woman I was telling you about, the director of the ensemble, Claudia Clybourn." Beau smiled at her, without a shred of subtlety, or guilt, and Claudia found herself struggling to smile and be gracious.

"Claudia, this is Adrian. I believe you spoke with him, or his secretary, on the phone."

"Yes. I was under the impression that you were the one who was enabling us to purchase the music to play this year. Thank you. I appreciate your generosity."

Adrian shifted uncomfortably, but his smile did not waver. "I'm so glad that a small town like Sweet Water has someone who can lead a group like this. Communities need this type of thing to bring them together. I love that you're volunteering your time to do that."

"It's been fun. I've had a really good time. And I think most of the people who are playing in it have been enjoying it as well. Thank you," she said again, not missing the fact that he did not acknowledge that she thanked him. Twice.

He said a few more things and then moved away, heading toward the front of the church and disappearing around the side.

"He was in town to visit with my dad. They're business partners. And I guess he wanted to stop in and see what was going on. I didn't notice that he popped in the back, but he said he did."

"I saw the door closing, and wondered about that, but I didn't actually see a person," Claudia said, but she was distracted. She didn't know whether to say something or not. But she didn't like secrets. She didn't like it when people kept them from her, so she could hardly keep them from someone else. "I heard what he said."

Beau's eyes slapped to hers, and a guilty flush stained his neck.

"You're angry."

It sounded like a question, but it was said almost fatalisticly, like he already knew the answer.

"No. I don't think so. You're funding the ensemble?"

"Yeah."

"Why? Why didn't you just tell me? Why hide it? I guess that's the thing that bothers me."

"When I started it, you and I weren't exactly on great terms. I... I think I was a little more fond of you than you were of me. I didn't want you to know, because I thought you might refuse the money, or think that I was doing it for some underhanded reason."

While she wanted to be upset, she had to admit that he was absolutely right. She might have jumped to the exact wrong conclusion, and his fear was absolutely legitimate.

"I can hardly be mad at you when you're completely correct."

"I didn't mean it as a slam."

His hand touched her shoulder, carefully, almost as though he were afraid she was going to shrug off his touch. As if. She stepped closer.

"I know you didn't. I..." She smiled a little, looked away, and then said what was in her heart, even if it did sound a little bit corny. "You have a heart of gold. I know that. Now. You're right. Back then I probably didn't, but...I know that your motive would have been pure.

You've been nothing but kind to me since we actually started talking instead of trading insults."

"Yeah. I've been meaning to tell you, I just, how do you say, by the way, I'm doing this. It felt like bragging, you know?"

"If you're doing something good, and you say it, it's not bragging. It's just the truth."

"Well the Bible says that we're not supposed to go around bragging about all the good deeds we do."

"But you can tell me where the money is coming from." She paused. "Are there any other secrets you're keeping from me?"

"Maybe one. Or two."

"Really?" She felt her eyes getting big, as she drew back a little, as far as his hand would allow. It exerted pressure on her shoulder to stop.

"I'll spill those too if you want me to."

"All right?" she said, bracing herself. What in the world else could he want to tell her?

"We spent a lot of time together in the last two months. Most of it working, not a whole lot of talking going on, but I've gotten to see you in everyday situations. I... I love what I see. I love you." He took a breath. "We talked a little bit about how I didn't want to kiss you until I knew for sure that what we had was going to be more. I don't know about you, I don't know how you feel, but I couldn't be more sure that you are the one for me. The one that God has for me, the one I'm supposed to be with. Whether it's on my ranch, or on yours. I know we had that conversation, and I thought later that I don't care wherever we are, as long as we're together. It doesn't matter to me."

"I just talked to my family. I told them that I didn't want to leave them, but I felt like I should, and they agreed that it seemed to be true that God was nudging me in your direction."

"You've already talked to your siblings about that?"

"I didn't want them to be mad at me. I knew I needed to say something, and it felt like the right thing, me going to you. Us on your ranch. Maybe... Maybe we can still help with the singing in the evening?"

"Absolutely."

She stepped closer, putting a hand on his chest and sliding it up to his shoulder.

Then she paused. "There was something else?" Her breath caught as she remembered that he had said there were two secrets.

"Yeah. It's kind of related to the first one."

"Okay?"

"I told you I loved you, and... I guess you know I've been thinking about kissing you for a long time. I... I decided tonight that I was going to ask if it was okay."

"Okay to kiss me?"

"Yeah."

She couldn't help the smile that spread across her face. She reached out, and cupped his cheek with her hand. "I love you too. And I would love for you to kiss me. I feel the exact same way. This is the last relationship I'll ever have."

"Yeah. Same." His voice was just a murmur, as he lowered his head and his arms slid around her, and he kissed her, their breath mingling, the world falling away, and the sensation of everything fitting perfectly into place. She was right where she was supposed to be, kissing the man she was meant to marry, and loving him as much as her soul would allow.

He lifted his head. "Marry me?"

"Yes!" she said, smiling. She hadn't really pictured her marriage proposal, but if she had, it probably wouldn't have been like this, behind the church, after ensemble practice, after being totally petrified that the man she just said yes to was hiding things from her, but she realized that sometimes the way she pictured things in her head was the exact wrong way, and the way they actually happened was the exact right way. This was one of those times. Everything was perfect as he lowered his head and kissed her again.

Epilogue

Lucas stood in front of the library door, fingering the books in his hand.

This time, when he went in, he was going to pay attention to the books that he was picking out. He wasn't going to pick out something about the love life of earthworms, or seven thousand ways to use earwax, or knitting sweaters out of dogs' hair, and making money from those products. No, he was definitely going to pay attention to the books, and be sure that he didn't get anything more embarrassing.

But he also determined that this time, this time, he was going to say something to Ryland. The last eleven times he'd been in the library, his tongue had uncharacteristically stuck to the roof of his mouth. He wasn't used to that, but he wasn't going to allow it to happen again. He would speak to her, ask her...something. Out on a date, maybe, or just talk about the bacteria that lived in a person's eyebrows or about the fact that a person swallowed two spiders per lifetime in their sleep. Or not. No. He'd talk about something totally normal. He'd be funny and engaging, the way he always was with everyone else.

Ryland did not have to render him speechless. Again.

With a determined set to his shoulders, he opened the library door and strode in.

~

Join Jessie's list and be the first to know about new releases and sales on her books!

Read *A Cowboy's Gentle Touch*, the next book in the Sweet View Ranch series featuring Lucas and Ryland. Lucas' interest in obscure books somehow leads to a disastrous date with the shy librarian, but somehow they keep coming back for more. When a panicked decision puts their relationship in jeopardy, will Ryland save her cowboy hero?

Sneak Peek of A Cowboy's Gentle Touch

Lucas Clybourn took a deep breath as he put his hand on the library door and opened it.

He'd been in the library eight times since Christmas, and each time, he'd intended to ask the librarian, Ryland Solomon, out on a date.

Each time, he chickened out. Today, *today* was going to be the day that he actually did what he had been planning to do and ask the woman out.

It shouldn't be that hard. It's not like she was going to talk back to him or anything. After all, he wasn't sure he ever actually heard her say anything. At least not to him. Other than "may I see your library card please?"

Which, he had to admit, no one could say in a more sultry or romantic tone. It had given him goosebumps the whole way to his toes and back.

Cold North Dakota wind blustered down the street, and he hunched his shoulders as he pushed the door open.

The library opened three minutes ago. He'd been sitting in his truck for over fifteen minutes, waiting. He'd done the chores on the farm early, made sure the water was not frozen, and headed into town.

He didn't want there to be any other patrons in the library when he asked Ryland out. He had a feeling she might turn him down.

But the eight trips he made in the last two weeks surely counted for something. After all, that proves that they had something in common, right? Hefting the heavy armful of books he intended to return, he set them on the cart and walked further in, past her desk.

She stood at a display, her no-nonsense skirt falling below her knees. It was a librarian-colored navy blue, and the leggings she wore looked thick and heavy. As did her boots. They weren't heeled or stylish. They were flat and square, and they looked very warm.

She had a bulky sweater on. It was another library-dark color, and while it was not skin tight, it fell to her hips and emphasized the straightness of her slim figure. Her wavy hair, a dark brown color, fell to the middle of her back.

She moved slightly, and his eyes caught on her fingers, long and slender and very adept at arranging the books on shelves.

His heart started stuttering in his chest, and his feet slowed to almost a crawl, but she did not turn around.

Ryland Solomon was not exactly known for her effusive, bubbly personality.

That was him.

Except around her, he got all tongue-tied and couldn't seem to think of a single thing to say any time his eyes landed on her. It was like looking at her turned off the speaking part of his brain.

It also made his throat dry, and his tongue wanted to stick to the roof of his mouth.

Which was crazy, because he didn't have that reaction around anything. He was fearless, loved people, loved talking to anyone, loved being friends with everyone, and loved it when people loved him.

Maybe that's what made Ryland so interesting to him, because typically he didn't have a problem getting people to smile at him, talk to him, chat about anything with him. He could talk about literally anything.

Except with Ryland.

He didn't really think it was the challenge that drew him to her. Maybe it was the fact that she was so opposite from him.

He'd moseyed past her, and she hadn't lifted her head at all. It was like she knew it was him and didn't want to talk to him.

Normally he didn't have those kinds of thoughts. He didn't take anything personally and just assumed the best about people, automatically, without having to try to get himself to do it at all. It was just something he naturally did.

He sighed, walking to the first tall shelf and moving around it, paying no attention to the books on it, and trying to think about how he could find an excuse he could use to go back and say something to her.

She was a librarian. She could answer a question about a book.

Of course.

He grabbed a book from the shelf and walked back toward her, his steps slowing as he approached. She didn't lift her head to look at him at all.

"Is this a book you would recommend?" He held up the book he'd grabbed from a shelf.

She looked up at him and blinked. He didn't know how long she looked at him, but it felt like an eternity. Maybe a second or two. But still, that second or two dragged on and on and on.

Finally, she looked down at the book in his hand and tilted her head a little, maybe so it wasn't quite upside down and she could read the title better.

Without looking up, she began to speak. "*The Complete History of Public Farting. Everything you want to know about passing gas in public.*" She looked up, and there wasn't a smidge of humor on her face. "There are some books in this library that I have not read. That is one of them."

She waited maybe a breath longer, and then she turned back to her shelf.

So... Maybe it was the whole pride going before a fall. Or maybe it was just because he was a total idiot. But he had just thought he could talk to anyone about anything, but he had since found that there were subjects that he could not talk about with this serious and taciturn librarian. Public gas, its history and complete subject matter, was one of those things.

He could not think of a single thing to say.

He couldn't even get the words *thank you* out of his mouth.

Time ticked on, and he felt extraordinarily uncomfortable. Did he go back to the shelf and pick up another book to ask her about? Or did he decide he was going to check this book out anyway?

Every time he visited the library for the last eight times, he'd got at least eight books out. This would mess up his plan, and she might suspect that he was in here for something more than just picking up books.

"So, uh..." He cleared his throat. "Miss Solomon. Could you recommend a book for me?"

Man, he was such an idiot. If he was going to shove words out of his mouth, why didn't he say, *Miss Solomon, would you go out on a date with me?* Since that was the whole reason he was here.

She finished shelving the book in her hands and then picked up another book, holding it in both hands and twisting it a bit, slowly and carefully, as though she were thinking. "Typically when someone asks me to recommend a book to them, I ask what their interests are. However, since the last eight times that you have been here, you picked up books on rocks, the moon, alternate forms of psychology, competitive dog grooming, extreme ironing, and your fiction titles have included *The Great Gatsby*, the *Iliad*, *Middlemarch*, *My Best Friend is a Werewolf*, *The Man Who Could Not Kill Enough Fungus*, *The Secret Life of Jeffrey Dahmer*, and *Fifty Shades of Purple*."

He held up his hand. "That one was a mistake."

She raised her brows, and he immediately closed his mouth, feeling like the teacher had reprimanded him in front of thirty other students and slapped his fingers.

"Given that there has been such a wide range of titles from you in less than two weeks, books which you could not possibly have read before you returned them, I have to say that I couldn't and don't have a clue where your interest might or might not lie, and the only recommendation that I could potentially give you would be from the psychology section, and specifically, several books on bipolar disorder."

Right. So, he'd impressed her. He was pretty sure he'd impressed her.

"Would you like to go on a date?" So there, he got it out. So clunky and so unlike his typically suave deliveries. She was going to turn him down flat. He braced himself.

She looked back up at him, her brows high, her face a honeyed mask of absolute disdain. "The library is open late on Fridays and Saturdays. I would have to do it on Monday."

"I'll pick you up at six."

"My bedtime is at eight."

"I'll see you then." He thought maybe that was going to be the end of it, and he needed to hurry out so that he could do his fist pump and happy dance, without her noticing, then she added, "The psychology section is right over there."

"That's okay. I'll just take this one."

He held up the book in his hand and started walking toward the door.

"Just because I agreed to go on a date with you does not mean that you do not have to check that book out, sir."

"Oh. Yes, ma'am." He turned back around and stood at the desk.

She arranged two more books before she left her display and went to stand behind her desk. "You really ought to bring your library card, and then you can use the electric scanner in order to check out your books."

He almost said, *but then I wouldn't get to talk to you*, but he didn't. He didn't want to do anything that might jeopardize the fact that he had convinced her to go out with him.

Except, he hadn't really convinced her. She just said the absolute truth about him, because he was pretty sure he remembered most of those titles, not reading them, because he didn't actually read, but he did remember checking them out.

Honestly, he just went through random shelves in the library, pulling books and trying to catch glimpses of her over the top of or between the shelves.

Of course, there was the mess in the back of the library, shelves that needed to be put together, shelves that needed to be fixed, and a whole section of drywall that needed to be replaced because of the leak that happened last summer. He had avoided that section, even though it was the best area to get a glimpse of her since there were no shelves in the way.

He was so busy thinking about those things that she had his book checked out, handed it back to him, and walked away from her desk before he managed to think about getting his mouth moving.

He'd never met anyone that made him speechless. How did she do it? And as he watched her no-nonsense stride back to the display, he couldn't help but admire her. She...was so calm. Beyond his nervousness, beyond the fact that he couldn't get his mouth to work when she was around, there was a sense of peace that surrounded her, that drew him more than anything he'd ever noticed in a person before. How could she be so indifferent toward him? And how could he admire that so much?

Well, at least he had a date with her. Although, for the first time in his life he was going to have to practice speaking, because he didn't want to sit across the table from her and have absolutely nothing to say. He'd never done it before, but he could write a cheat sheet of things that he could talk about, in case his brain went blank as it had a tendency to do when she was around.

Yeah. That's what he'd do. There would be no long, awkward silences on this date. He was going to wow her and knock her socks off, and... He really didn't know where they would go from there.

Sign up for Jessie's newsletter! Get a free book, access to exclusive bonus content, get fun and funny updates on her life on the farm and more!

A Gift from Jessie

View this code through your smart phone camera to be taken to a page where you can download a FREE ebook when you sign up to get updates from Jessie Gussman! Find out why people say, "Jessie's is the only newsletter I open and read" and "You make my day brighter. Love, love, love reading your newsletters. I don't know where you find time to write books. You are so busy living life. A true blessing." and "I know from now on that I can't be drinking my morning coffee while reading your newsletter – I laughed so hard I sprayed it out all over the table!"

Claim your free book from Jessie!

www.ingramcontent.com/pod-product-compliance
Lightning Source LLC
Chambersburg PA
CBHW060316310726
48976CB00007B/2342